Something To Read On the Plane

© Jan Hurst-Nicholson 2006
First published in 2006 by Writers' Circle Publishing,

2nd impression 2007
Reprinted 2009
Reprinted 2013

www.just4kix.jimdo.com

ISBN 0-9584978-4-2

Cover design and illustrations by:
Jill Nicholson (no relation)
Cover illustration by:
Gail Gillings

Typesetting: Helen Osborne
Layout: Helen Osborne and Ivan Littler

The stories contained in this book are works of fiction. Names and characters are the product of the author's imagination and any resemblance to any persons, living or dead, is entirely coincidental.

All rights reserved. No part of this publication may be reproduced, stored in a retrieval system, or transmitted in any form by any means electronic, mechanical, photocopying, recording or otherwise without the written permission of the author.

Something To Read On the Plane

A Bit of Light Literature, Short Stories & Other Fun Stuff

Jan Hurst-Nicholson

Published by

Writers Circle Publishing

Jan Hurst-Nicholson has been published in a wide range of magazines in SA and overseas and is also the author of several children's books:

- *Leon Chameleon PI and the Case of the Missing Canary Eggs* published by Gecko Books
- *Leon Chameleon PI and the Case of the Kidnapped Mouse* published by Gecko Books
- *Bheki and the Magic Light* published by Penguin SA
- *Jake* published by Cambridge University Press
- *The Race* – an inspiring story for left-handers

Jan Hurst-Nicholson has also published:

- *The Breadwinners* – a family saga

- *But Can You Drink The Water?* – a humorous novel

- *Mystery at Ocean Drive* – a teen action adventure

- *I Made These Up* – short stories for the fireside

- *With the Headmaster's Approval* - fiction

Contents

A Quick Word – foreword

World **W**ide **W**orry
A Night on the Run
A Matter of Convenience – *short story*
Something in the Air
The Great Ant War
Poste Haste – *short story*
Malapropisms
A Fine Kettle of Fish
Technically Speaking
Doctor's Orders
Light's Out – *short story*
Dear Agony Aunt
Down the Hatch
Sex Education Ain't What it Used to be
The Tryst – *short story*
Purrfect Communication
A Violet Headache
Night Noises – *short story*
Fifty Reasons for Feeling Fifty
The Letter – short story
Technical Tantrums
How Friendly a Passenger are you? Quiz
Flying Doctoring
One Little Pig Stayed at Home – *short story*
A Public Inconvenience
Household Aids
Sticking Together
Family Ties – *short story*

To Eileen, my mentor - who's always willing to 'just check this through for me.'

A Quick Word
(hardly anybody reads a foreword)

A comprehensive survey conducted by email, in dentists' waiting rooms, and surreptitiously watching incorrigible magazine readers who do their reading at magazine counters, revealed:

- Readers like the back page humour, the letters, and the Agony Aunt column.
- Those with two-second concentration spans prefer one-paragraph snippets.
- People who buy the magazines for the articles settle down to enjoy the short story with a cup of coffee and a fag.
- A percentage of men trawl through anything looking for boobs and bums (if you fall into this category try The Tryst and Sex Education)

These revelations inspired this volume of preferred reading matter, i.e. give the readers a bit of what they fancy.

My quest was then to find a publisher who would fall for it, and subsequently sell enough copies to provide regular Lotto-sized royalty cheques.

If you have actually paid for this book then my theory was correct and the money will flow in. If you are merely browsing, cracking the spine and putting sticky fingerprints on the pristine pages, then beware - you could be under surveillance.

WORLD WIDE WORRY

The Internet has opened a whole New World for the hypochondriac. Whereas medical knowledge was formerly limited to magazine articles, health books and know-all neighbours, the Web is a virtual Disease City, providing a magnitude of frightening medical possibilities.

Hypochondriacs do not worry alone, they also diagnose for friends and relatives, which is why Health Sites receive tens of millions of hits annually, and may indicate that hypochondria is contagious.

It is fortunate that my Auntie Phoebe is not still around to log on. Auntie Phoebe suffered from every disease known to woman (and, occasionally, man). She was jealously possessive of her infirmities. Whatever ailed friends, neighbours and relatives, Auntie Phoebe was also a martyr to. This included problems with her 'prostrate'. We even invented a disease – retillion – that she swore had left her kidneys permanently impaired.

Auntie Phoebe prided herself that her symptoms were more severe, unusual or previously unknown to that disease. She liked nothing more than to baffle the doctors. Papers were going to be written about her, like dispatches from the front. She was a challenge to medical science.

Auntie Phoebe's unhealthy interest in medicine began in her younger days when she spent two years as secretary to a gynaecologist. The doctor's handwriting required Auntie Phoebe to look up spellings in a medical dictionary – which, happily for her, also provided a description of the disease. Her escalating medical knowledge sometimes emboldened her to pre-empt the doctor's diagnosis, and patients would enter his office secure in the outcome of their visit. It was not long after that Auntie Phoebe's employment was terminated.

When she left the practice, Auntie Phoebe had amassed a sizable quantity of medical journals, an out-of-date Mims, and the happy knack of steering every conversation down the avenue of medicine. She gathered together symptoms like a data bank. A veritable *www.tellauntyphoebe.com* she could surf Mims – on the hard drive inside her cranium - for answers to any medical conundrum.

If someone arrived at the comforting conclusion that his or her medical problem would disappear if certain vitamins were imbibed, Auntie Phoebe would gleefully trawl her memory, and quicker than any search engine would suggest the symptoms indicated a more menacing disease. But she was also *www.auntiephoebewillfixit.com*

Auntie Phoebe knew about party power long before Tupperware. Like a dating agency she would match her friends' symptoms and then hold coffee morning pill swaps. Pills for a bad back would surely help ease the pain of sciatica. A nervous disposition would benefit from anti-depressants. As far as we know, no one died as a result of her ministrations.

Aged 92, Auntie Phoebe died peacefully in her sleep. Nobody would have been more surprised than she next morning.

At the wake, her family ceremoniously threw the Mims on the fire. I thought it was a pity. I had been hoping to look up causes for my sore throat.

Never mind there's always the Web.

✈

A NIGHT ON THE RUN

There is never a good time to get the trots. And a long weekend in a full caravan park is definitely not one of them.

I'm no gastronaut. I like my food plain, and avoid anything on the menu that has to be explained. So I put it down to the take-away salad. The olives to be precise. My wife, who had generously given me her share, had not become similarly afflicted.

It was 21h30 when I became uncomfortably aware that my digestive system was not all it should be. I crawled miserably into the sleeping bag.

By 22h30 cramping pains warned that serious internal mischief was afoot. Like a caterpillar emerging from a cocoon I slithered out of the sleeping bag and clambered over my gently snoring partner. Torch in hand I unlocked the door and stepped into the inky blackness. A sullen yellow light glowed dimly from the ablution block. I tiptoed along the gravel path, fearful of waking slumbering neighbours.

Feeling a slight sense of relief I re-emerged into the darkness, only to suffer a near relapse when a spectre-like figure loomed out of the shadows and manifested itself before me. A low growl announced the welcome presence of the security man and his trusty canine partner. We nodded companionably and he was swallowed up in the night.

I'd hardly settled back into the sleeping bag when internal rumblings forced a repeat trip, this time requiring a little more alacrity. I tried negotiating a shorter route between neighbouring vans, but a netting of guy ropes and lethally positioned steel pegs had me blundering about like a myopic hedgehog. I barely made it in time. The dreaded Diarrhoea &Vomiting was upon me.

I hoped that no one else had partaken of the olives. This was not the time to be forming queues.

I needed liquids. But my wife, having been advised to treat all water with suspicion, had added judicious amounts of sterilising fluid to our storage tank. It was like drinking swimming pool water. I opted to risk it straight from the tap. If anything scurrilous lurked in its contents it wouldn't linger long enough to cause any further ill effects.

As midnight approached I was prancing back and forth like Michael Flatley on speed. The guard dog's growl had now turned to a wag of recognition and I considered including him in my holiday snapshots.

For the sake of convenience, I gave up closing the caravan door. If someone came in to murder me they would be welcome. The torch was coming out in sympathy, its beam as weak as I felt. I lay motionless in the sleeping bag, afraid even to cough.

I am not one to suffer in silence. I find it comforting to give the occasional groan, interspersed with whimpers of self-pity. My wife, usually the epitome of solicitous sympathy during the day, does not take kindly to having her sleep disturbed.

"Must you make those noises. There's no point in both of us being awake all night."

I groaned into a pillow before setting off on yet another excursion. It had to be dysentery at the very least.

A further encounter with the security guard had me mentally adding him to my Christmas card list.

By the feeble light of the torch I searched through my wife's medical Pandora of insect repellents, plasters, cough lozenges, massage oil for stiff muscles, headache remedies and sun block. There was nothing remotely suggesting a cure for D & V. Caravan parks are not known for their proximity to emergency chemists, and it would be pushing neighbourliness to knock on caravan doors at 04h00 expecting a lift into the nearest town. I curled up on the floor and awaited death.

As the sun gradually nudged in a new day I was mentally ticking off the people who could be expected to attend my funeral.

It wasn't long before the smell of fried bacon and sausages was drifting nauseatingly on the morning air.

My wife, refreshed after a night's sleep, was all loving concern. She brewed up an Oral Rehydration Salts solution of sugar, salt and water, and even cut the crusts off the slice of dry bread that was all I could face.

It wasn't long before fellow campers heard of my predicament. Ever helpful, they rallied round and came up with a selection of remedies. Weak, but continent, I lived through the day.

My wife, suffering sympathy fatigue, vowed there would be no more take-away salads. Bottled water was top of the shopping list.

I spent the rest of the weekend thumbing through the 'Guide to Caravan Parks', determined the next resort we visited would have private ablution facilities.

A passenger whose travelling style
Was to sit with his feet in the aisle
Caused those needing the loo
To complain to the crew
Who provided them all with a stile

A MATTER OF CONVENIENCE

Family holidays were not the happy events they had once been, especially now that Walter's bladder had become a liability.

"Let's go this way. It's a short cut." Mavis angrily mimicked Frank's words under her breath. Short cut to what? The next ruddy life by the looks of it. There was no chance of making a dash for it. Not that her Mam was up to dashing anywhere with *her* feet. And the only time her dad moved faster than a slippered shuffle was when he'd overdone the senna pods.

She wrung her hands in anguish. Trust Frank to stall the car in the middle of the ruddy lion enclosure. The midday sun was blazing down and the car was already like a sweatbox.

"Try it again, Frank," she fumed.

"It's no good. The battery's flat."

"That's your fault? You've known about it for weeks. This isn't a car park. You can't just hop out and push. Not with them lions."

Frank was about to remind her that the only reason he'd looked for a short cut was to get her Dad to the lav, but he was interrupted by a plaintive voice from the back.

"Hey, our Mavis. Why've we stopped?" Walter had been regretting that second cup of tea even before they'd entered the safari park.

"Car's stalled," muttered a scowling Gerry, wedged sullenly between his grandparents in the back seat.

"That wasn't very clever, Frank," Gert told him, prodding his shoulder with a bony, arthritic finger.

Frank winced. He cast around for signs of a game ranger, or other visitors foolhardy enough to venture out in the stifling heat. But they were alone. Except for the lions, eyeing them expectantly from the shade of a tree.

Mavis glanced furiously at her husband. He'd done this on purpose. She knew it. He was just waiting for her Mam to say "I'm never going nowhere in this car again." That'd be all the excuse he needed. And our Gerry too. They both hated these family holidays. Sometimes she thought they hated her Mam and Dad as well.

"Let's try rockin' it," said Frank. "Might get the connections touching, or start it rolling. There's a bit of a slope. Everybody jump up and down."

The car squeaked and groaned under an onslaught of uncoordinated bouncing, pitching and rolling like a rudderless yacht in a turbulent sea. But it remained stubbornly immobile.

"Hang on, hang on," said Frank, calling a halt. His wheezing in-laws sank back like punctured barrage balloons.

"Try the starter again," urged Mavis.

The click was almost deafening.

"Let's have another go at bouncing, but with a bit of rhythm this time," said Frank. "When I say go, we'll all jump up together."

But Walter and Gert were still gathering their wits when they should have been up. The family resembled a set of rather wobbly and badly-aligned pistons.

"Useless, this is," muttered Walter, a light spray of spittle drifting from his badly fitting dentures onto Mavis's bare neck.

"I'm opening the window, our Mavis," announced Gert, sucking loudly on a Rennie. "The heat's getting to me."

"But Mam, we're not supposed to…" Mavis began hesitantly.

"I told you we should've gone to the beach," grumbled Gerry.

"Don't you start, m'lad," fumed Frank.

"Leave him alone, the lad's right," agreed Gert. "You was the only one who wanted to come here."

Frank swung round, rebellion rising. "I did it for you. To get you out into the fresh air."

"Fresh air! You call bein' in this car fresh air!"

"Stop it. Stop squabbling," cried Mavis, tears brimming. Why did these outings always end in a fight?

"Can't sit here all day," announced Walter, opening the door and clambering out.

"Walter!" screamed Gert.

"Dad!" echoed Mavis. "What are you thinking about?"

"All that jiggling up and down. It's made me want the lav even more," grumbled Walter.

"You'd know about wanting the lav with

17

that lion after you," muttered Frank.

Mavis grabbed her Dad's shirt and yanked him back in. But the sudden jolt dislodged his upper set and his gasp of surprise propelled it into a clump of long dry grass.

"Now you've done it," spluttered Walter gummily.

"Good, now he'll have to get a new set," said Frank. "Like a pair of castanets those old things were."

Mavis shot him a fierce glare. It seemed that the only time Frank spoke to her parents was to make a sarky remark. Why couldn't it be like it used to be, when Gerry was a kid and they'd gone to the Isle of Man on the ferry? They'd had fun together in those days. But that was before they'd had a car. Before they'd all been trapped together for hours on end.

Her thoughts were interrupted by Walter. "Hey up," he cried. "Look what's coming."

A lion, aroused by the noisy squabble, had slowly risen to its feet and was padding quietly towards them.

"Dad, close the door. The window, Mam, the window!" shrieked Mavis.

They stared in fearful expectation as the big cat circled them. It came unsettlingly close, regarding them with its suspicious ochre eyes.

"Don't panic. It can't get in," said Frank.

"Worra about me teeth," wailed Walter. "It'll have me teeth. Distract it, our Mavis. Throw it a cheese butty."

Frank's eyes rolled heavenwards. "It's a lion. Not a ruddy pigeon at the Pier Head."

"Our Tibby used to like a bit of cheese," muttered Walter, feeling sat on.

"Me Dad's only trying to help," snapped Mavis.

A full-scale fight was about to break out when Gert gave a wheezy moan. "I don't feel right," she whispered, a wavering hand clutching her throat. "It's me chest. It feels all tight."

"What's up, Gran?" sighed Gerry.

"It's me heart." She gave a weak cough. "I think it's me heart."

Frank and Mavis exchanged glances.

"Have another Rennie, Mam," said Mavis wearily.

With a pettish lip, Gert unwrapped the tablet. She was popping it into her mouth when Walter let out a shriek. "It's got me teeth, it's got me teeth."

The lion was taking an inquisitive sniff at the strange, odd-smelling object that lay beneath the car.

"Hoot, Dad. Hoot," urged Gerry. "You might scare it away."

Frank blasted the horn. The lion gave a momentary start, took a final sniff, and with a look of disdain, ambled off.

"Now's your chance," cried Mavis, her eye on the big cat as it retreated to join its mates.

"Chance to what?" said Frank.

"To nip out and get me Dad's teeth."

"Yer what! You want me to risk getting'

mauled for your Dad's choppers?"

"He can't spend the rest of his holiday with no teeth."

"Come on, Dad," pleaded Gerry, mortified at the thought of appearing with his Granddad minus his upper set.

Frank calculated the distance between car and lion. "All right," he relented, slowly opening the door. He slid out, cast an anxious eye at the lion and then bolted to Walter's door and began a desperate search in the long patchy grass. He spotted something beneath the rear wheel. But as he stooped to gather up the yellowing molars the car began a slow roll. He watched in fascinated horror as the wheel gradually crushed Walter's only means of chewing.

"Frank, the car, it's running away," screamed Mavis. "Gerrin' quick."

Wrung from a mesmerised trance, Frank sprinted after the moving vehicle. But his foot caught a tussock of grass and sent him sprawling. Temporarily winded, he heard the screams of his family entreating him to get up, only realising the urgency when he saw two lions trotting towards him. Leaping to his feet he hared after the car, reaching it as the big cats quickened into a lope. He jumped in, rammed into gear and let out the clutch. There was a collective sigh of relief as the engine spluttered into life.

"Thanks be praised," said Mavis.

But Walter wanted to know what had happened to his teeth.

"Yes, where's his teeth," complained Gert. "He won't want to be slurping soup for the rest of the holiday."

A red mist descended. "They're broke," said Frank through tweezer lips.

"They were good teeth, them were," lamented Walter, as the car bounced its way back onto the road. He cogitated on his loss for a while before announcing, "You'd better be quick getting to that lav."

"It won't be long, Dad," said Mavis, reflecting on the wisdom of these family holidays. Her Dad's bladder was becoming a bit of a liability, and her Mam's heart only played up when they were doing something contrary to her wishes. And then there was Gerry. The only thing that would please him would be if they all vaporised and he could go off on his own. Perhaps next year they'd send her Mam and Dad to Blackpool.

And then Gerry was announcing, "There it is, Dad. There's the café and toilets."

Frank swung the car into the car park and drew to a halt outside the public conveniences. But it was obvious that something was amiss. The entrance was blocked by bricks and bags of cement. An overalled worker was wheeling a barrow inside.

"What's going on?" asked Frank.

"We're closed. Renovations. You'll have to use the toilets on the other side of the park." Seeing Walter's anguished jiggling, he offered, "If you're in a hurry, you can nip through the lion enclosure. It's a short cut."

✈

SOMETHING IN THE AIR

An anxiety that haunted my childhood was the fear of catching a mysterious disease called '*something*'. Such were its powers that it could invade the body in a myriad of ways, and it lurked almost everywhere waiting to be caught by an unwitting host.

Something, according to my mother, bred and multiplied in all forms of dirt. It lurked in the soil and could enter the body through the soles of the feet simply by one walking about barefoot. It effortlessly found its way onto unwashed hands and then into the food of unsuspecting diners where it was known to cause serious internal trouble.

My mother was somewhat of an expert on the causes of *something* citing information extracted from *The Modern Home Doctor* (published February 1935 edited and specially written by MEMBERS OF THE MEDICAL PROFESSION illustrated by 16 plates and drawings in the text. Requirements for a healthy home: good construction, soap, hot water, elbow grease, and fresh air.)

These persons of the MEDICAL PROFESSION were known in the family as 'they'.

'They' advised – according to my mother – never putting your face near the cat. This was a guaranteed way of catching *something*. Eating unwashed fruit would produce a similar fate.

Other children were frequently carriers of *something* Wearing other children's shoes, drinking out of the same glass and most definitely using the same comb would result in a serious case of *something* and must be avoided at all costs.

Random bouts of *something* occurred on school camping trips when the washing of hands before meals was not strictly enforced, and stomachs had to adjust to suspect water supplies. Many children had their holidays aborted after having caught a nasty bout of *something*.

Something was especially prevalent, according to my mother, in public toilets. Virulent strains of *something* lurked on toilet seats and could be caught by simply sitting on the seat (rather than perform a balancing act, our family developed strong bladders and learned always to 'go' before leaving home.) Not only was there a danger from the seats, but also from ill-informed members of the public who didn't wash their hands after going to the toilet and therefore left *something* on door handles.

Eating establishments also had to be vetted. Those that my mother 'didn't like the look of' - principally hot dog vendors and dubious-looking seaside fish and chip establishments – were not patronised. She could not be pinned down to specifics, but as the authority on *something* and the one who had to deal with the consequences if one of us actually caught *something,* we knew better than to argue.

Something was also capable of skulking in clean and thoroughly hygienic areas. Wearing blouses or shirts, or even more seriously an item of underwear that hadn't received a proper 'airing' could result in pneumonia or *something*. The clothes-horse, with its freshly ironed clothes, always took precedence in front of our fire.

In 1950s England, foreign travel was quite rare. When travelling to Africa one was likely to catch rather exotic diseases such as malaria, or dysentery. However, countries nearer to home were rife with *something*, whose symptoms more often included diarrhoea and vomiting. A specific strain of *something* could, according to the MODERN HOME DOCTOR be attributed to 'taking unsuitable or indigestible food', which my mother translated into 'eating all that foreign muck'.

These days, except for sporadic outbreaks of '*something* going round', it has either died out or mutated and given way to grander sounding afflictions such as gastro-intestinal disorder, which commands more respect than the anonymous *something*.

Thanks to my mother's vigilance, we rarely caught *something*.

But childhood fears often lie dormant. Whenever I experience unexplained symptoms I think of my mother and wonder if, after rubbing noses with the cat, I may after all have contracted *something*.

✈

THE GREAT ANT WAR

My husband awoke at three a.m. with burning feet. As consciousness surfaced he realised it was something more than gout. ANTS! His feet and legs were alive with the tiny black creatures. So was the bed. It was like an Alfred Hitchcock - *The Revenge of the Ants*.

He leapt into the bath and hosed off the swarming mass while I stripped the bed. The affronted cats, disturbed from their slumber, watched in amazement as we vacuumed the scurrying insects from over and under the mattress, and followed their trail to the point of entry on the windowsill. This was now WAR.

It had begun the previous summer as a series of small skirmishes. Being Eco-friendly – poor ants, they're only looking for food, they're part of nature's plan - I had tried all the sympathetic routes of eradication.

When they attacked the dogs' food, I placed their dish in a tray of water. The ants detoured round the tray and up onto the kitchen counter. I sprinkled basil leaves under the back door. They came through the kitchen window. I blocked their way with talcum powder. They went up the outside wall, into the roof and entered via the kitchen light switch, which made alarming fizzing and hissing noises when switched on.

I hosed the ants off the wall and, slightly less Eco-friendly, put a room-fogger in the roof. Battle lines were drawn with *'miraculous insecticide chalk'* around possible entrances. They swarmed in through the electrical wall sockets.

Life with the ants was becoming tiresome. A pinhead of biscuit crumb would, in nanoseconds, be surrounded by a platoon of scout ants. Pets had to be frisked before they were allowed indoors. Tiny corpses of dead ants had to be swept up. At least one half-hour of every day was dedicated to the elimination of ants.

Alarm bells sounded when I discovered them coming up through the wooden skirting, a length of which they had hollowed out. These ants, I should point out, were the tiny black kind, not the termite variety, and could reduce a dead gecko lizard to a skeleton in a matter of hours.

Becoming even less Eco-friendly, I began with the *Dyant*. But they were too cunning. They found their way in through the bedroom air-conditioner. We opened the wardrobe one morning to discover a seething black mass swarming over our clothes and shoes. Our entire wardrobe was removed to the garden. Like demented semaphore signallers, we shook the ants off.

They made it impossible to sit in the garden. And in single file, like a circus high-wire act, they made their way along the clothesline to the freshly laundered clothes. Swatting them off the damp washing resulted in clothes speckled with tiny black bodies.

There was little sympathy from friends. A lifting of the shoulders, a bemused look - ants – so what? Until I chanced upon a fellow sufferer. We fell on each other's shoulders, swapping horror story for horror story, each one eclipsing the next. Ants had felled one of her precious trees. They had blown the circuit board of her neighbour's automatic gates. They had nearly devoured her husband during the night, leaving him with an eye infection. The doctor was unconvinced that ants could have cause inflamed puncture wounds. We were united in our nightmare.

We contacted knowledgeable parties. An ant expert advised that these ants could be of the carnivorous Argentinean variety, the Pit Bulls of the ant world; enemies of our local ants. With no need to be Eco-friendly, we brought in the big guns - *Chlorpyrifos* and a large spray gun.

A vigilant daily inspection and spray regime brought them down to manageable proportions. There were a few minor skirmishes when they found their way in through the airbrick under the bath, but the ants got the message.

Or perhaps they've headed next door, I'm sure I heard a shriek coming from there.

✈

POST HASTE

Frank heaved a sigh of relief when his wife's relatives went home. Little did he know his troubles were just beginning.

As Frank watched the plane finally lift into the South African sky he allowed his hands, teeth and buttocks to gradually unclench. Three weary months of his in-laws were at last over and they were safely on their way home to Liverpool.

He had nursed secret doubts that he'd ever be rid of them. Only hours before take-off panic had broken out when Walter had once again mislaid his false teeth. "I'm not going nowhere without me teeth," he'd announced, gums stubbornly set. But for once his absentmindedness was not to blame. They had been found in the kitchen where Gert had put them to soak in a cup of mild bleach solution.

Hunched beside Frank in a misery of post-holiday mourning, Mavis sniffled her regrets into a sodden tissue. "I wonder when we'll see them again. They're in their seventies you know. And what with Aunt Lil being taken, so sudden like…"

Frank's eyes rolled back. Aunt Lil had been a bone of contention, or more precisely a charred bone of contention ever since his in-laws' arrival. "You've brought what with you?" Frank had spluttered, staring in outraged disbelief at the shiny ceramic tobacco jar.

"You heard me – yer Aunt Lil," confirmed Gert, tweezer-lipped.

Restraining himself with difficulty, Frank watched his mother-in-law place Aunt Lil's ashes beside the red pottery cat atop his new telly.

And so Aunt Lil had remained a member of their touring party; Gert's chinking reminder of the suddenness of death whenever Frank was tempted to exceed the speed limit.

They drove home from the airport in cautious silence, punctuated only by Mavis's sniffles, plagued by a misguided guilt that by immigrating to South Africa she'd wrenched their Gerry from his devoted grandparents.

Frank smiled a secret smile. Stretching luxuriously before him lay an evening in his own chair, a pristine newspaper, and command once more of the telly remote control.

Twenty minutes later he sank gratefully into his chair and switched on the television. But his newly discovered happiness was short-lived. For there, spotlighted by a shaft of winter sunshine, sat the shiny tobacco jar.

A red mist descended.

"Worra we gonna do Frank?" wailed Mavis through streaming eyes. "Me Mam'll go spare when she finds she's left our Lil behind.'

Frank thought for a moment before deciding. "We'll put her in the post."

Mavis gave him an uncertain look. "Can you do that? She wrung her hands in anxious doubt as she stared at the remains of her relative. "What happens if the jar breaks?"

"We won't send her in the jar. We'll put her in an envelope."

Mavis had misgivings. "I don't know, Frank. It seems sorta disrespectful." And then, suddenly afraid. "Maybe there's a law against sending ashes in the post?"

"We won't tell 'em what it is. We'll wrap her in birthday paper and let on it's a present."

"But what happens if they find out we've been fibbing? They might confiscate her. What would I tell me Mam?" Distraught at the thought of Lil being impounded Mavis allowed fresh tears to flow.

"They haven't got time to open every parcel," Frank reassured her. "Get the postal rates and one of them customs forms you kept from last Christmas."

Mavis, a weepy and reluctant accomplice to what might be a criminal offence, set off in search of the relevant forms.

Frank carried the jar to the kitchen, holding it with the trembling caution of an altar boy caught in a cross draught with a flickering candle.

He took out the kitchen scales and set them down in readiness.

"Worra you doing?" asked Mavis, returning with the forms.

"Weighing her," said Frank, the jar poised over the empty scale pan.

Mavis was outraged. "You can't tip Aunt Lil into a scale pan as if she's half-a-pound of self-raising!"

"Why not?" asked a disgruntled Frank. "We have to know how much she weighs for the postage. What d'you want me to do – anoint the bloody scales first?"

Mavis threw him a look that would have withered a giant redwood. "You could've lined it with a bit of paper first."

Frank was not keen on bits of Aunt Lil contaminating the next batch of bread pudding, Frank allowed Mavis to spread a piece of greaseproof over the scale pan, reverently, as if she were conducting a religious ceremony.

"Careful," she chided as Frank heavy-handedly spooned the last few ashes in. "We don't want her blowing about the kitchen."

"Just over a kilogram," he announced. Consulting the postal rates, he carefully removed a spoonful and then re-checked the scales.

"What d'yer think your doing?" demanded Mavis.

"It's extra if you go over a kilogram," explained Frank with aggrieved logic.

"And just what do you propose doing with the surplus spoonful?"

Frank's gaze wandered to the rubbish bin.

"Oh no you don't. That could be a foot or a hand you've got there. You put it right back, Frank Turner!"

With a resigned shrug, Frank tipped the ashes back into the scale pan just as a sudden draught gusted through the window. For a few blustery seconds grey dust floated about the kitchen like holy dandruff before quietly settling on Mavis's shiny Dri-Brite floor.

Frank reached for the Dustbuster. But Mavis was across the room and wrenching the machine from his startled grasp. "What's the matter with you?" she spat out the words through clenched teeth. "It's my Aunt Lil, not your bloody ashtray."

"I was gonna put her back," he offered lamely.

"Together with the biscuit crumbs and cat hairs I suppose!" Using a pastry brush, she carefully swept up the scattered ashes while Frank rummaged for an envelope.

Taking pains to disturb the ashes as little as possible, Mavis carefully slid Lil's remains into the envelope and gave it a little pat to more evenly distribute the contents.

Frank was busy with the forms, filling in the 'description of contents'.

"You can't put that," she choked. "Free gift. No commercial value."

"Why not?"

Mavis was horrified. "What'll me Mam think? It sounds awful. And what's more, they'll chuck her away if the parcel goes astray." This was a new fear. "I want to insure it," she suddenly decided.

"Insure it! For how much? Its replacement value? And how d'you know they're Lil's ashes. They could've come from someone's grate for all we know."

This was too much for Mavis. Her Mam and Dad gone, and now this new worry. She burst into fresh tears.

"Come on, Mavis," coaxed Frank, giving her a hug. "We'll insure it if that's what you want."

But Mavis wouldn't be consoled.

"Tell you what," said Frank. "I'll phone the funeral parlour. Maybe they'll know what to do."

Mavis thawed and the gasping sobs were reduced to a sniffle. It would be best to do it proper. Maybe the funeral people had a courier service, or someone to look after it, like they did with children and elderly people.

The undertakers proved sympathetic and promised to make suitable arrangements for Aunt Lil.

Let's hope that'll be the last of it thought Frank, filling the kettle for a good cuppa. But his eye was suddenly attracted to a lone teacup sitting forlornly on the draining board. Oh no, it couldn't be. He glanced into the cup. It was. There, set in a malevolent whiter-than-white grin, lurked Walter's false teeth.

✈

MALAPROPISMS

The accidental misuse of words have become known as 'malapropisms' after Mrs Malaprop, a character in Sheridan's play, *The Rivals*, and can be collected daily by astute observers.

1. The beggar held out his hat hoping someone would throw their spare penis into it.
2. **After some argument, Lisa finally copulated.**
3. Malcolm decided to break the eyes by offering him a drink.
4. **George helped himself to a crusty junk of bread.**
5. A low rummage began to form in the dog's throat.
6. **He bought a sexual title flat.**
7. She began to divulge in her favourite daydream.
8. **A healthy meal is sausage or mash or worse.**
9. She stared as if she'd been memorised by his eyes.
10. **They were having a wail of a time.**
11. She stared into the coal-black debts of his eyes.

12. "I don't want to," she said, pursuing her lips.
13. I'll take some cough medicine to dilute my lungs.
14. I watched him in my review mirror.
15. They developed a warm plutonic friendship.
16. For a happy marriage a man needs a co-opted wife.
17. He brought back a gift as a momentum of his friendship.
18. Have a Merry Christmas and a Phosphorous New Year.
19. The snake looked like a boa constructor.
20. He was a millionaire magnet.
21. She gave him a prognostic look.
22. It was Hoptions choice.
23. You must put out the garden refuse.
24. You've got to be more pacific.

25. This muesli must be old, it's got weasels in it.

26. He can't be there himself. He's going to dedicate one of his men to attend.

27. She let herself into a small dinghy office.
28. **He went as white as a sheep**.
29. We got on like a horse on fire.
30. **I had a flat feeling – an anti climate.**
31. Once he hit me, I had to repatriate.
32. **We went at it hammer and thongs.**
33. The news came like a blot from the blue.
34. **The tumour turned out to be malicious, but the cancer is now in recession.**
35. Think of him as a protective angle without wings.
36. **A good speech should be sprinkled with appropriate antidotes.**
37. We need a weekly cleaning rooster.

See following page for key

KEY TO MALPROPISMS

1. penis – pennies
2. **copulated – capitulated**
3. eyes – ice
4. **junk – chunk**
5. rummage – rumble
6. **sexual – sectional**
7. divulge – indulge
8. **worse – wors**
9. memorized – mesmerized
10. **wail – whale**
11. debts – depths
12. **pursuing – pursing**
13. dilute – dilate
14. **review – rear view**
15. plutonic – platonic
16. **co-opted - cooperative**
17. momentum – memento
18. **Phosphorous – prosperous**
19. constructor – constrictor
20. **magnet – magnate**
21. pragnostic – pragmatic
22. **Hoptions – Hobsons**
23. refuge – refuse
24. **pacific – specific**
25. weasels – weevils
26. **dedicate – delegate**
27. dinghy – dingy
28. **sheep – sheet**
29. horse – house
30. **climate – climax**
31. repatriate – retaliate
32. **thongs – tongs**

33. blot – bolt
34. malicious – malignant, recession – remission
35. angle – angel
36. antidotes - anecdotes
37. rooster – roster

A FINE KETTLE OF FISH

At holiday time there are kennels for dogs, and even hotels for parrots. But for fish - there are only neighbours. Two small boys had entrusted me with the care of their loved ones. As I stared apprehensively into their tank, two goldfish and a couple of disinterested snails peered sulkily back. It was going to be a long three weeks.

On the second day I noticed the water lacked its previous sparkling clarity. Never mind, didn't goldfish lead healthy enough lives in garden ponds?

By day three the water had taken on a decidedly murky hue. I had been instructed to take out two cups of water daily and replace them with fresh water. However, a jug had been left for this purpose. Perhaps I had misheard and I should have been replacing two jugsful daily. It took quite some skill removing a jug of water from the small tank without capturing fish, snails, and marine foliage.

By day four the fish tank resembled a scummy pond. Tiny frothy bubbles were bursting and reproducing like fermenting beer. The snails were nowhere to be seen. I feared the fish could be gasping their last.

I made tentative enquiries about fish replacements, but feared the children may have had an unfortunate knack of recognising their pet's idiosyncrasies. Could have taught them synchronised swimming, or darting through hoops. Surrogate fish would be exposed as impostors.

Quelling a rising panic, I sought medical assistance.

"Does the water smell?" enquired the vet.

I gave it a sniff. "Yes, definitely stagnant."

"Do the fish have scales?"

"What? I thought all fish had scales."

"Do they have white scales?"

I couldn't say, I could hardly see the fish through all the murk, let alone their scales.

"They could be suffering from ich?" he murmured.

"Ik, ick? What's that?"

"A disease that fish are prone to. You've probably been over feeding them. The food has rotted and fouled the water."

Thoroughly alarmed I asked how I should remedy the situation.

"Place the fish, water, stones, shrubbery etc into a clean, detergent free bowl. Clean out the tank, refill with water and allow to stand for 24hrs before replacing the fish."

"What about the snails?" I asked.

"Are the snails all right?"

How does one tell? Snails don't do much in the way of activity on which to base an opinion.

"Do you want the snails?" he persisted.

I didn't know. After all, they weren't actually *my* snails. Could be a home industry set up by older son, breeding them for a local restaurant. Or younger son's biology experiment. I opted to keep them.

In order to clean out the fish tank I would need a receptacle in which to temporarily house the fish. The only vessel of a suitable size was the fish kettle. I hoped it would not have a damaging psychological effect on the fish.

I scooped out the fish with the jug, but the snails revealed a stubborn streak by clinging tenaciously to the side of the tank. They required a prod with a wooden spoon before releasing their grip.

As I heaved the tank into the sink and poured the dirty water down the plughole a large quantity of the tiny stones that covered the base disappeared with the water. The possibility of blocked drains was added to my worries.

The following day I was relieved to find the goldfish were not the floating corpses I had feared. But as I transferred the aquatic menagerie back into the sparkling clean tank, I was alarmed at finding the addition of several long, thin, worm-like creatures of a strange orange hue. Could they be important aquatic wildlife vital to fish survival? I consulted my husband. A quick glance. "Fish shit," he pronounced.

There was no way of confirming this nugget of fish wisdom.

I set the tank back on the kitchen table and peered smugly through the shiny glass. Two sets of eyes peered pitifully back, their mouths opening and closing like starving fledgling birds.

I couldn't help myself – I reached for the fish food.

✈

TECHNICALLY SPEAKING

As a child in the 1950s, illnesses had a vagueness that made them somehow less fearful.

My aunt had a 'bad' leg. It was known in the family as *Maud's leg*. "We can't walk too far with *Maud's leg*." It meant trips had to be curtailed. I felt it rather unfair of *Maud's leg* to misbehave in this way.

Uncle Fred, on the other hand, had a 'bad' heart. I thought of the hearts displayed in the butcher's window and wondered if Uncle Fred's heart had 'gone off', as my mother reckoned those of the butcher often had.

Also excused long walks and lengthy standing was my friend's mother who 'suffered with her feet'. She wore a pained expression and bedroom slippers with holes cut in the side to relieve her bunions.

Suffering was quite common. A neighbour 'suffered with her nerves' - a mysterious affliction that seemed to imply some sort of inadequacy on her part (as opposed to today's less blameworthy 'stressed out' or legitimised 'panic disorder'.) It never occurred to us that by endlessly bouncing tennis balls against her bedroom wall we might be contributing to the 'nerves'.

But these problems sounded no more alarming than a bruise or a cut finger.

My first experience of a serious illness was my grandmother's 'upset stomach', which at first sounded as though it had been mildly offended, like a maiden aunt being cheeked by the grocer's boy. Certain foods disagreed with it. I frequently heard its grumbling objections as the internal conflict took place. But one night something must have tipped it from upset to very cross as she was rushed away by ambulance.

The frightening word 'haemorrhage' drifted through my closed bedroom door and for the first time I was struck by a fear of illness.

Disorders of a serious nature were never discussed in front of the children. These were conducted discreetly in hushed tones in order to afford the ailment the respect it deserved.

Medical confidentialities were often exchanged while waiting in the grocer's queue. Nuggets of medical information fell my way as the bacon was being sliced. "Mrs Armitage is under the doctor again with her chest." "Mabel's husband's got trouble with his water-works." "Me husband's got problems with his back passage. I've told him it's from sitting on those radiators."

If the grocer himself were present, delicate disorders of a female nature were extravagantly mouthed. "She's got problems *down below*."

Although these snippets conjured up rather bizarre images, they were not unduly alarming. Euphemisms and understatements served a useful purpose in saving the listener the true horrors of the complaint.

My friend's bedridden grandfather, who was several times at death's portal, was never described as more than 'poorly'. Except on the occasions his Yorkshire sister visited when his condition deteriorated into 'proper poorly'. Inquirers were spared the graphic details of his daily existence, unlike today when every symptom and bowel movement is recounted to strike terror in the listener.

Medical science has come a long way since the 1950s. With it has come a greater awareness, knowledge, and unfortunate openness that compels patients to share the intimate details of every infirmity in gruesomely frank detail, even to those of us who would rather not know.

If you wish to remain a medical innocent you should avoid asking, "How are you?" This once formal greeting has now become an invitation for a lengthy medical history.

Some of us would welcome a return to the vague but all encompassing 'indisposed'.

✈

DOCTOR'S ORDERS

"You're suffering from stress," the doctor told my husband. "Take a relaxing holiday."

"I've bought a caravan," announced the patient.

"You've what! All that housework in miniature."

Undaunted, my husband towed the second-hand Sprite Alpine home in triumph. Until we reached our driveway.

The brick gatepost and its pergola picturesquely shrouded in bougainvillea appeared fractionally lower than the caravan, even to my untrained eye.

"The sun roof will have to come off," proclaimed my husband.

The driveway has a steep incline with an immediate left sweep and a high retaining wall on the right, so this seemed a sensible precaution. Off came the roof and on to the 'to do' list went 'raise the pergola'.

"You'll need a rally awning," an experienced caravanner advised. We practised erecting it on the brick driveway, wrestling the poles like two cub scouts with an enormous troop flag.

We tested the 'fridge and stove. Like two

kids playing house we made ourselves tea and viewed the neighbourhood through the unfamiliar aspect of the caravan windows.

We were ready for the big day.

Up at 06h00. Hitched and all set at 07h00. Jammed against the gatepost at 07h05.

The law of mechanics that allowed the van entry was now mystifyingly preventing its exit. The right-hand wheel dipped on the curving slope causing the van to tilt at a sharp angle and engage the gatepost with a disconcerting grating of metal.

My husband's first priority when confronting a problem is to establish that it's not his fault.

"You could see. Why didn't you tell me!?"

"I was watching the wall. I can't be both sides at once!"

Ill-humour hung in the air. The stress barometer nudged up several degrees.

Reverse gear was engaged. Five year's worth of tyre tread transferred itself to the driveway. The van remained cosily tucked against the gatepost.

"We'll have to jack it," snarled my husband. Up went the caravan. The car, like a clever levitation trick, rose to join it. With back wheels no longer in complete contact with the ground there was a sense of forward movement. I shrieked a warning. Down went the jack to the loud accompaniment of scraping metal as the van re-engaged contact with the gatepost.

My husband, by this time dancing a little jig of fury, yelled, "Bricks! Bring bricks!"

Muttering mutinous oaths and watched by a gathering audience of curious schoolchildren, I grudgingly demolished my decorative lawn edging. Bricks wedged behind the wheels, the van hiccuped a few metres back up the drive.

"We need a ramp," was the verdict. Discarded bits of plank were added to the bricks until they resembled the beginnings of a mini Masada

Still hovering under a cloud of blame, I awaited the second attempt.

This time, after a frantic pantomime of directions, it was well clear of the gatepost, but fetched up against the retaining wall.

I steeled myself for the yelps of accusation. But visibly restraining himself in the presence of an audience, my husband inspected this further complication.

In went the jack. Muscles strained. Turning a delicate shade of puce my husband manoeuvred the van to a more agreeable position. Free at last.

The onlookers, robbed of a more interesting outcome, shuffled off to school.

Within a short while we were cruising towards our destination.

As we relaxed on the banks of a lagoon with its fishing, swimming and sailing, the stress barometer was soon registering zero. Just what the doctor ordered.

I wonder what he'll recommend for the hernia?

✈

LIGHT'S OUT

Tom enjoyed his job, even if it was a bit boring and predictable. He liked the routine and today was going to be an ordinary day – just like all the others.

"Me? Fired, sir!"

Tom Shelton replaced the receiver with a feeling of utter disbelief. It had started out such an ordinary day.

It usually took Tom a while to warm up after coming in out of the icy wind at the start of a shift. He huddled closer to the miserable one-bar electric fire that served to warm the cramped lodge. As he glanced out of the window he noticed a lorry dropping a porta-loo cabin on the pavement outside. He turned to young Alec, "I wouldn't fancy having to nip outside to a porta-loo in this perishing weather," he said, rubbing his hands together to get the circulation going.

"Might be nice working outside for a change. It does get pretty monotonous stuck in here all day," said young Alec, bent over the report book as he studied the night shift's notes.

"Not for me. Settled I am, see," explained Tom, filling the kettle from the tap in the tiny sink. "I like routine." He found it reassuring, one day the same as the next, reporting who went in and who came out. Complacent, Eileen said he was. But what reason was there to be anything else with a routine job like this?

The gate bell buzzed. "I'll go, you see to the tea," said Tom, already half way to the door. He unhooked the clipboard and picked up a pole with a mirror attached. A delivery van was spewing exhaust fumes next to the gate. "Morning," said Tom cheerily, handing the clipboard to the driver.

"Morning, Tom," replied the driver, scribbling details on the yellow form.

Tom opened the doors at the back of the van and routinely peered inside. Finding nothing untoward he proceeded to check the under parts of the van with the mirror. "OK," he said, adding his signature to the form on the clipboard. He signalled to Alec, the gates swung open and he waved the van through.

Returning to the lodge he poured his tea and took it over to the window. Two men in yellow oilskins were setting out red traffic cones. A van drew up and disgorged three more yellow-jacketed workers armed with spades and jackhammers. "Wonder what they'll be digging up this time," he mused.

"Whatever it is, there'll be potholes left in the road," muttered Alec cynically, joining Tom at the window. The workmen helped to relieve the tedium. There usually wasn't much to look at, apart from the bleak factory walls opposite, with their occasional splash of graffiti, and the distant smoke stacks.

Tom took another gulp of the sweet tea, finding pleasure in the home comforts of the tiny office.

Outside, the men were leaning on shovels and pickaxes, woolly Balaclavas pulled over their ears to keep out the biting wind. The pickaxes were heaved into the air and brought down with a thump, and the first chunks of tarred surface were wrenched from their bed.

"Here we go," said Tom, "another patchwork road." He fetched the gingernuts he kept for his morning cuppa and was dipping one contentedly into his tea when the jackhammer started up, juddering and shuddering in the trail of the pickaxes.

The gate bell buzzed again and Tom reluctantly started towards the door. A black Mercedes was purring at the gate. "Must be the nobs come for a conflab about tomorrow's move," said Tom, unhooking the clipboard .

He touched his cap as he handed the board to the driver, who filled in the form with an impatient scrawl. The gates swung open and the car swept hurriedly through. Tom shrugged. He didn't make the rules.

After a while the noise of the jackhammer ceased. The men lit a primus stove and brought out packets of sandwiches.

Tom was transferring the details of the yellow forms into the report book when there was a tap on the window. A Balaclavered man held up a blackened kettle. "Got any water, mate?" he yelled through the thick glass. Tom signalled for him to go round to the gate and unplugged the electric kettle, still three-quarters full of hot water.

He held the spout between the railings and poured the hot liquid into the battered kettle. "Ta," said the man, nodding the woolly hat. "This'll speed things up. Kettle takes forever to boil on that primus."

"What'yer digging up now?" asked Tom conversationally.

"New sewers. These old ones can't cope with you lot," the man replied with a grin.

"They only talk it here," said Tom, laughing.

The man strode off, chuckling to himself.

As the day progressed the trench steadily lengthened. Soon a mound of untidy rubble had formed. At noon the men downed tools and the woolly hat re-appeared with his kettle.

"I expect you'll be glad to keep busy in this weather," said Tom. "Must be cold sitting about."

"Thermal underwear, that's the secret," confided the woolly hat. "We're used to waiting about for stuff to be delivered. I expect the pipes will arrive just before knocking-off time, and that'll mean working overtime to unload them."

Tom thought it would be a while before they'd be ready to lay pipes. They'd only taken the top surface off. But he smiled encouragingly. "Rather you than me," he said, remembering that tonight Eileen would be making his favourite – steak-and-kidney pudding. Feet up by the fire and watching the telly after a good meal, that's the life.

That reminded him. With a satisfied smile he unwrapped the neatly packaged sandwiches

Eileen had made. Roast beef and chutney today. He offered one to Alec.

"No, thanks. I'm going to heat up a tin of baked beans," replied Alec, toasting a slice of bread in front of the electric fire.

A real home from home, this is, thought Tom, switching the kettle on.

Several vehicles came and went before the woolly-hatted foreman re-appeared at three o'clock for more water. "Still no sign of the pipes?" enquired Tom.

The man shook his head and glanced at his watch. "He'd better be here soon, or we'll be leaving him to unload on his own."

An hour later, just as the winter dusk was setting in, Tom saw a lorry weighted with heavy concrete pipes draw up at the road works. "Woolly hat'll not be pleased," he muttered.

The lorry was mounted with a crane, which proceeded to unload the pipes with the assistance of heavy chains and the shouted instructions and curses of the foreman.

As the pipes swayed in a perilous arc the men scrambled to safety to watch with stamping feet from a distance, hands shoved deep into their pockets.

"Taking it very high, he is. Hope he knows what he's doing," observed Tom.

"Who is?" asked Alec, strolling over to the window.

"The bloke on the crane. He nearly had that lamp post down then." They stood in companionable silence watching the huge concrete pipes being lowered to the pavement.

The streetlights suddenly flickered into life. But instead of dispelling the gloom, they cast eerie shadows that enhanced the cold and misery in which the men worked. "You were right," said Alec, "we're lucky to be working in the warmth. It doesn't do to take things for granted."

The crane cranked back and forth in the gloom and Tom lost interest and returned to the report book to fill in the last few entries before the end of the shift.

"Last cup of tea, Tom?" said Alec switching on the kettle. "Warm you up for the walk home."

"Good idea. Need something to keep me feet warm."

With that there was a crash and the streetlight flickered several times and went out, plunging the workmen into darkness.

Tom peered out, rubbing the condensation from the window with his sleeve. The woolly-hatted figure of the foreman materialised. "Light's out," he shouted through the glass.

Taking his fleece-lined coat from his locker Tom shrugged it on and ventured into the cold night air. "What's up?" he said.

"That silly bugger of a driver almost knocked down the lamppost. He's smashed the top. Light's out. Can I use your phone to report it?"

Tom hesitated. It was against the rules to allow anyone into the lodge. "Look, I can't let you in, but I can make the call for you," he said,

"That'll be OK. Here's the number." The foreman took a scrap of paper from his pocket and scribbled down some figures. "Tell them Jake phoned and the light's out."

"Will there be someone there at this hour?" asked Tom doubtfully.

"Twenty-four hour number," said the foreman. "Don't forget – light's out."

It sounded a bit cryptic to Tom, whose past experiences with the corporation switchboard was one of being passed from department to department. Nevertheless, he dialled the number. A man swiftly answered and Tom passed on the message, adding his own rider that they'd better be quick about fixing it.

"The 'guvnor' won't like that light being out tonight. Not with tomorrow's transfer," Tom told Alec. "Anything goes wrong with that and someone's head will roll."

It was five minutes to the end of their shift when the alarm bells jangled. At the same time the telephone shrilled in the lodge. Tom picked it up. It was the angry chief officer.

Rodney Light, due to be transferred to a high security prison the following day, had escaped into the darkness by climbing into a sewer pipe lowered over the prison wall.

Funny, the things you take for granted.

✈

DEAR AGONY AUNT

There was a time when nearly all women's magazines had an Agony Aunt, and it was one of the most eagerly read columns. But they were able to answer only a few of the thousands of letters received. Some people were beyond help.

Dear Aunty,

Next week my husband and I will be celebrating our 50th wedding anniversary. All our married life, when my husband wants to make love he says, "Let's put the lights out and not go to sleep, eh?" this not only drives me mad, but it also turns me right off sex.
Do you think now would be a good time to tell him?

Wondering, Sleutelfontein

Dear Aunty,

My parrot has been pulling his feathers out until he is almost bald. My neighbour says it's because I let the parrot see me in the nude and this makes him sexually frustrated.
Do you think parrots can be trained to close their eyes?

Bird Lover, Noordhoek

Dear Aunty,

I spend a lot of time travelling with my job, while my wife stays at home to look after our children. I have noticed that my younger son looks very like the man next door. Do you think this is because my son spends a lot of time playing at my neighbour's home?

Uneasy Father, Kroonstad

Dear Aunty,

I am a 45 year-old woman who wants to breed her Pekinese. A man answered my ad in the newspaper and we arranged for him to bring his male dog to cover my female. The man told me he needed encouragement and we should show him what to do. The man made love to me on my bed, but his dog would not even look at my bitch.

The man said that perhaps his dog could not see properly from the floor and suggests that we try again, but next time we have the dogs on the bed with us so that his dog is sure to see exactly what is required.

Do you think the dog's claws will damage my satin quilt?

Houseproud, Olifantsfontein

Dear Aunty

The man next door has a mango tree that is level with my first floor bedroom window. Every night when I am undressing I see him in the tree. He says he is picking grubs off the immature mangoes and if I leave my bedroom curtains open the light will help him to see the tiny grubs.
If I leave my curtains open for him do you think he will give me some of the mangoes when they ripen?

Chutney Lover, Pinetown

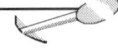

Dear Aunty,

I am a 16 year-old virgin. My boyfriend wants to make love to me. He says if I put a paper bag over my head and don't see what happens I'll still be a virgin.
Do you think it will make any difference if I use a brown paper bag or white paper bag?

Puzzled, Trompsburg

Dear Aunty,
We are five typists in our twenties who all have boyfriends. Our boss is a 55 year-old spinster. Every time we talk about our boyfriends she disappears into her office, sits scribbling on a piece of paper, and then rips it up. When she went out one day we took the paper out of the rubbish bin and painstakingly pieced it together. She had written ALAN, over and over again.
Do you think we should report her to the senior manager for wasting paper?

Concerned, Benoni

DOWN THE HATCH

"I can't. It's too big."
"But you'll have to. The doctor told you to."

This, and similar exchanges have haunted my life. As a child I used to get cooing sympathy, but now I just exasperate everyone. They can't understand how the simple act of swallowing a pill, capsule or tablet should be such a trial.

My mother wearily accepted my troublesome handicap, although I think she was partly to blame. She banned gob-stoppers and chewing gum on the grounds that accidental swallowing would result in a medical emergency. My throat muscles were now panicked into instantly rejecting anything remotely umasticated.

To stave off winter ailments she resorted to subterfuge. Cod-liver oil capsules lurked in the mashed potato. Haliborange tablets masqueraded as Smarties and I was frequently offered spoons of strawberry jam flecked with a mysterious white substance, suspiciously like a crushed tablet. Food became a minefield of medication.

My affliction accompanied me through school and college to my first job where a minor ailment took me to the clinic. I glumly returned to the office with a course of tablets.

Despairingly I confronted the medication, which seemed to have grown from tablet to lozenge proportions. My colleagues gathered round to offer advice. "Just put it on the back of your tongue, take a mouthful of water and swallow."

They watched in eager anticipation. I felt like the final number in the lottery draw.

I gulped down the water. "Has it gone?" they asked expectantly. Head bowed, I confessed the tablet was still clinging limpet-like to the back of my tongue.

Exasperated groans. "It must be something to do with having had my tonsils out." I pleaded.

"Rubbish," was the general response.

Initial attempts left me water-logged but otherwise unharmed. But by the fourth try the sugar coating had begun dissolving and the tablet's terrible innards were released. Communication was reduced to shuddering Aaghs and Ughs as I quaffed a Niagara of water.

Trapped in hospital for a short spell I soon learned that busy nurses have better things to do than coax problem pill-swallowers. Two torpedo-sized capsules sat clammily in my hand. I suggested to the nurse that she go away and assist with a transplant to give the medication time to complete its pilgrimage to my stomach.

She made an impatient explosive sound. A matron in training, she was obviously used to dealing with awkward customers. Apparently I could be suffering from pnigophobia – a fear of choking. Not the kind of phobia that could be treated with large doses of anti-anxiety pills.

Although my foible was legitimised, it did not make her any more sympathetic. Embarrassed at delaying vital medication to the rest of the ward, I did the only thing possible – I chewed the capsules. The repulsive contents exploded into my mouth, paralysing my taste buds. I choked down the water. It was too much to hope for a sweetie or a spoonful of jam.

At least no one need be overly concerned that I could become a substance abuser, or for that matter, do away with myself with an overdose of sleeping pills. I mean, one hears of people swallowing a bottle of pills, but has anyone ever chewed their way through one?

Although I've never had to take medication on a regular basis, I have experimented with vitamin pills. Vitamin A and E capsules are readily chewable as they have no particular taste. Iron tablets aren't too bad, except that they are very hard and I'm never quite sure whether the crack is a tooth, or the tablet breaking. The B tablets are rather nasty and will never become an acquired taste. But the hands-down winner is the 1000mg Vitamin C. Sucking a lemon would be a positive pleasure by comparison. And I did have one 'chew and swallow' failure. A fibre tablet, which claimed to do miracles for the digestive system, swelled like oat bran on steroids leaving me with a mouthful of sawdust.

I have to confess though; there was a time when I thought I was cured. Maybe it was systematic desensitisation, but a course of the contraceptive pill gave me renewed determination.

Placing the tiny pill on my tongue I took a large swallow of water and couldn't believe it – the pill had actually gone!

I was ecstatic. It was akin to when I managed my first couple of swimming strokes. I walked smugly about for several days as if I had joined some exclusive club.

This is the start of something big, I told myself. Alas, 25 years on nothing larger has slipped down my gullet. I'm still chewing, and what's worse, it would seem that pnigophobia runs in families. My Maltese terrier SPCA special stubbornly refuses to swallow her worm tablets!

✈

> A passenger thought a good ruse
> Was to travel without any shoes
> The stench from his feet
> Cleared the neighbouring seat
> So perhaps it's a ruse we could use

SEX EDUCATION AIN'T WHAT IT USED TO BE

Give a baby a puzzle that requires placing different shapes into their corresponding apertures and the mother will say: "Don't show him, let him work it out for himself, it will be more educational." That just about sums up sex education in the 1950s. The sexual revolution had not even cranked into first gear.

We learnt about sex in a 'pass the parcel' method, each experience unravelling a little more of the mystery and bringing us closer to the ultimate. We weren't quite sure what it was, but knew it to be awe-inspiring otherwise it wouldn't be known as 'Having it off' or "Getting your oats."

Today, films and magazines are awash with sex. It's even taught in schools. It wouldn't surprise me if it became a matric subject – that would take the fun out of it!

In our slow fumbling way we certainly had a good time learning – and plenty of laughs at the mistakes and misconceptions (!) of our fellows. I believed that babies came from women's boobs, and in the case of twins, one from each boob. My grandmother was torn between agreeing with me (which could lead to untold problems in later life) and offering the correct explanation. My mother rescued her by suggesting a nice cup of tea.

Our parents, who mistakenly believed that if we didn't know about sex we wouldn't indulge in it, carefully censored our viewing and reading. If the television threatened to go beyond the kissing stage my mother would switch it off and announce her intention to 'write up' about all the filth they were putting on.

Our sex education was limited to whisperings in the schoolyard, and the occasional snippet from my friend, Susan. My mother was not happy at the source of these snippets. Susan was not only herself born out of wedlock, but lived with an older sister and cousin who were similarly disadvantaged. My mother worried that I would 'catch' illegitimacy from the family. Much to her relief, my friendship with Susan was severed when I moved up to High School.

Here we were handed a book entitled You Are a Young Woman Now (it was an all-girls school). The book clearly explained menstruation, and touched lightly on babies, i.e. it showed them in the womb, but offered no explanation as to how they got there.

But High School divides the innocents from the not-so-innocent and our group included one non-innocent. For the price of a chocolate digestive her exploits could be heard in a corner of the schoolyard during breaks. Knees tucked under chins, buttocks riveted to the freezing concrete floor, we listened in shocked disbelief. Had one of us been brave enough to ask for clarification on certain points the discourses would have proved more educational.

It was from my friend's married sister that we first learned of contraceptives. My friend had not swallowed the balloon story and had eventually been told the truth. We mulled this information over, passing it on to fellow pupils, some of whom gasped with sudden understanding – they'd also been told about the balloons.

Then Lady Chatterley's Lover hit the headlines. Four hundred girls lined up to read the one copy that someone had filched from an older brother. The 'good pages' had been conveniently marked to speed things up.

The sexual revolution was getting into gear.

A type of Berlin Wall separated our school from the boys' side. A request to be allowed out at lunchtime was firmly turned down by our Headmistress on the grounds that 10 years previously a boy and girl had been found together in compromising circumstances. This meant that love letters had to be smuggled between the schools by the few girls who went home for lunch. Those lucky enough to be recipients of these lusty missives would have a giggle of friends gathered about them like ferrets round a rabbit hole. All the letters began exactly the same. DO NOT SHOW THIS LETTER TO ANYONE. As letters were regarded as status symbols, this request was rarely acceded to.

One letter mentioned French kissing. A brave soul asked: "What's French kissing?" We all laughed at such naivety while listening avidly to the explanation.

Sex was all done by numbers. Kissing was number one; French kissing number two, and so on through to ten. The day after a party would find groups of whispering girls feverishly trying to out-shock each other with rumours that so and so had 'gone to number seven, or even eight'. I knew that three and four had something to do with touching above the waist, but was unclear as to the rest.

At 14 years we made the acquaintance of a farmer's son. We immediately volunteered our services as farm hands. Here, amongst the bales of hay, I received my first real kiss.

By now we all knew the fundamentals of how a baby was conceived. After a prolonged discussion we agreed that touching above the waist would be safe – but definitely no further.

When boyfriends began knocking on the door my mother's warning of, "Now you be careful crossing the road," was suddenly shortened to, "Now you be careful!" emphasised by a wagging finger. She never spelt out quite what I should be careful of – but I knew, and she knew I knew.

At 16 years I moved on to a mixed sex college. It was here that I learned about homosexuals – queers in those days. My mother did not know what a queer was. I told her it was a homosexual. "Oh," she said, hurrying off to make a cup of tea.

The innocent kiss in the hayloft had now been replaced with the more erotic tremors of arousal. Our hormones were kicking in. Self-control became all-important. But in pre-pill days the fear of pregnancy was an effective inhibitor; the social disgrace alone would have been mortifying.

Then I met a guy who was known as the local virgin exterminator. With much trepidation I accepted a lift home. I was very relieved when he accepted that "No" meant "No'. We later became good friends and a group of us often went camping together. You can learn much about sex from sitting and quietly observing a bunch of guys boasting of their conquests. I was amazed to hear a rather prim girl described as the 'local bike'. I also discovered a tendency to exaggerate.

It seemed that once boys got wind a girl would 'go all the way', she became fair game. Fragile male egos would not accept a 'no' if they knew their mates to have had a 'yes'. If you'd slept with one, the likelihood was that you'd sleep with the rest.

Women's magazines were now discussing sex, and the Pill was launched. The swinging sixties were upon us. Fear of pregnancy was no longer a factor. But to some of us, going on the pill smacked of premeditation and was likely to put one on the road to becoming the 'local bike'. It would also have set us off on a sexual package tour; having seen and done the lot in the shortest possible time, but left feeling vaguely dissatisfied.

The generation that began the sexual revolution are now themselves parents of nubile daughters. I'm grateful I'm not a parent. Sex homework is the one subject which I'd hate to be told: "But we don't do it like that anymore."

✈

THE TRYST

Liverpool, England 1970s

He tried nibbling her ear. He wasn't sure whether he should be licking, nibbling, or kissing it. Even after re-watching a movie he still hadn't been able to make out the exact technique.

"Are you sure we can't be seen from the path?" Pam whispered, snagging her gymslip on a bush as she peered into a gloomy clearing.

"'Course not. I've staked it out. It's quite private." Colin assured her, settling on a grassy patch.

Pam, unsure of the next move, inspected the damage to her clothing,

"Sit down," invited Colin. "We can use our satchels as pillows."

Pam sat mutely beside him, knees tucked under her chin and encircled with her arms. In the expectant silence the late afternoon sunlight filtered through the trees. It was eerily quiet until Pam sighed and turned resignedly to Colin. "Well, what happens now? It's up to you to start." She flicked her long dark hair in an effort to look sexy.

He gripped her shoulders and pulled her lustily towards him.

"Hang on," she said, pushing him away.

"What's wrong?"

"Aren't you going to get rid of that chewing-gum first?"

"Sorry." He spat out the offending gum and tried again. " Come on, lie down. It's more comfy."

Pam lay back and clasped her hands behind her head, a move she'd practised to better reveal the outline of her budding breasts. Colin gently brushed her lips with his. She sprang upright as if stung.

"What's wrong now?"

"This grass is damp. I can feel it right through my knickers."

"Here, lie on my blazer." He hastily placed it under her bottom.

He tried nibbling her ear. He wasn't sure whether he should be licking, nibbling, or kissing it.

Even after re-watching a movie he still hadn't been able to make out the exact technique.

Pam lay unresponsive, her eyes closed. He was about to attempt a love bite when she unexpectedly turned her head and gave him a rather painful bang on the nose.

"What homework have you got?" she demanded.

Colin rubbed his nose in a violent effort to stop his eyes watering. "Just maths. Why?"

She giggled. "Funny they never give us homework when it's sex education."

"Perhaps they'll give us a 'do-it-yourself' manual when we leave school," grinned Colin, furtively unbuttoning her blouse. He gradually slid his hand inside, hardly daring to breathe lest Pam should object. His mouth was drying up, partly from excitement, but mostly because he was afraid to breathe through his nose in case it made him sniff.

"Colin, do you love me?"

"Course I do."

"How much?"

"Lots."

"Prove it."

"How?"

"Do my geography homework."

"Geography! You know I hate geography!"

"There. I knew you didn't love me," she said, removing his hand and sitting up.

"Okay, okay, I'll do it," panted Colin, whose hand had almost reached her bra. Satisfied, she lay back and allowed Colin to slip his hand inside her blouse again. She began to wriggle and heave her buttocks. Colin couldn't believe his luck. "Are you enjoying it?' he whispered, pressing eagerly against her.

"Enjoying what?" she asked scornfully. "Something's biting me bum."

Colin, somewhat deflated, hunted fruitlessly for the offending insect. "Must have been a piece of grass. Lie down again," he ordered.

She glanced at him quizzically. "You're not going to tell anyone about this, are you? If our David finds out, he'll kill you. He might even tell me Dad."

"Don't you trust me? I love you. This is something beautiful between just the two of us." He'd read that in a book. He kissed her, wondering whether he dare try a French kiss, thinking it might distract her while his hands sought their target.

Her bra was unfastened and he eased it up to expose two ripe, young breasts. Breathlessly, he stared down at them, half-expecting Pam to object. Encouraged by her silence, he tentatively touched one. Pam shrieked in alarm.

"What's wrong?" He hurriedly withdrew his hand.

"Your hands aren't half cold."

"Sorry." He rubbed them together before cautiously trying again. "Warm enough now?"

"It's all right."

He moved his hand experimentally. "Hey, look, your nipples are standing up.

"So what."

"So that means you're aroused."

"What do you mean – aroused?" There was a hint of disdain in her voice.

"Y'know, when a man's thing becomes erect it means he's aroused. Same with a girl. When her nipples are erect it means she's worked up."

"Doesn't make me feel any different," said Pam. "They go like that when I wash them anyway."

He was about to argue when she pressed her fingers against his lips. "Sshh," she cautioned.

"What's up?"

"I heard a rustle in the bushes. I think someone's coming."

"Well it's not me," said Colin.

"Shut up, stupid. It could be our David."

"There's no one there," Colin reassured her.

But Pam found something else to worry about. "Colin, how do you know I won't get pregnant?"

"You can't get pregnant the first time."

"Rubbish! Miss Marsh says that's a story all boys tell. It's a lie. You can get pregnant the first time."

"What does she know? What I meant was – girls can get pregnant if it's *their* first time, but if it's the *boy's* first time he won't make her pregnant."

"How do you know?"

"Peter Wilder made love to a girl last month and she didn't get pregnant."

Pam digested this new piece of wisdom. "D'you think Miss Marsh has ever, y'know, done it?"

"Doubt it," said Colin. "She's old. Must be at least thirty."

"Don't you think people over thirty bother anymore?

Colin considered his reply as he undid his belt . "My Mum was thirty-four when she had me, so they must have done it at least once after thirty.

Colin had unzipped his trousers. Taking Pam's hand, he was about to place it inside when she pulled away. "Come on, what's wrong now?" he implored.

"Aren't you going to take your shoes and socks off first?"

"Why should I?"

"My Mum says she can't stand men who make love with their socks on."

"But I've still got my shirts and trousers on. Why should I take my socks off?"

"Don't you want to take them off? Do your feet smell or something?"

"No, of course they don't," he said, resigned to exposing his bare feet. She watched while he wrestled with his shoelaces.

She made him feel stupid and he could feel the anger welling up. He grabbed her shoulders and forced her back on to the blazer, pinning her underneath him like he'd seen Clint Eastwood do.

"Ooh," she said, wriggling with delight.

"Do you like it?"

"Yes. You've got a huge spot on your neck with a big white head. Please let me squeeze it."

"No," he said, exasperated.

"Why not?"

"If it was Roger Moore you wouldn't be asking to squeeze his spots."

"Course not. Roger Moore doesn't have spots."

He glared at her. She glowered back defiantly. "Get on with it then."

He kissed her angrily, thrusting his tongue into her mouth while he fumbled under her skirt. Beads of perspiration broke out on his forehead.

"Colin, do you think I'm sexy?"

"Yes," he croaked.

She nuzzled his neck, avoiding the spot. "Are you sure you haven't done this with anyone else?"

"Course I'm sure."

"Perhaps that's what's wrong," she declared. "The man is supposed to be experienced so he can show the woman what to do."

"I know what to do," said Colin, unaware that anything had been wrong. "It's your fault. You're not reacting like you're supposed to." He circled her breast with his hand, stroking and squeezing. She stared at him with a bored expression. "See what I mean," he complained. "You're supposed to moan and groan and look as if you're enjoying it."

Pam contorted her face into feigned expressions of ecstasy. "Is that what you want? Heavy breathing and lecherous looks?"

"You're not supposed to sound like a steam train and look as though you're having an epileptic fit," Colin protested.

"How am I supposed to look then?"

"Like this," he said, producing a crumpled and well-thumbed photograph from his pocket.

Pam gasped in horrified fascination. "Where d'you get this? It's a porno picture."

"Gary Hewitt. When he showed it to Sylvia Wainwright it really turned her on." He waited for Pam's reaction. "She charges y'know," he added.

"Who does?"

"Sylvia Wainwright."

"How do you know?"

"Gary told me."

"You mean he paid her money?"

"No, she makes the guys do her homework."

"That's disgusting! It's cheap, like being a prostitute," said Pam.

She looked at him quizzically. "Are you sure you haven't been with her?"

"I told you I haven't."

"I don't know whether to believe you. My mother told me all men are liars, and never to trust them."

"But I love you. " He took her hand and cautiously moved it inside his trousers. Pam looked round nervously. "I don't like it here. It's spooky. I'm sure someone is watching us."

"Stop chattering," he demanded. "It's putting me off."

"Aren't we meant to talk?"

"It's supposed to be romantic – or just moans and sighs."

They were silent until Colin said, "Move your hand up and down."

"I can't. You're lying on my arm and it's gone dead."

Colin shifted his weight.

"What's the time?" she said, twisting his wrist to see his watch. "It's twenty to six," she gasped. "I'll have to be going or me Dad'll come looking for me."

"Just a few more minutes," implored Colin, whose body was throbbing painfully.

"No, me Dad'll kill me."

"But I thought we were going to be lovers," he wailed. "You promised."

"Perhaps next week, but not here, it makes me nervous."

"What about under the gym, next Thursday?"

"I'll think about it. You promise you won't tell anyone about this?"

"Of course I won't," he said, reluctantly dressing. "You'd better leave first in case there is someone around."

Pam sneaked away through the shrubbery. Colin watched her go and then waited as six schoolboys emerged from the bushes. He took a book from his satchel and checked the names against those of the boys. "Right, pay up," he said.

"Hey, look here, Colin," said a pimply-faced red-head, "I'm not paying the full amount. I hardly saw anything."

"That's your fault," replied Colin. "You chose where you wanted to watch from. Pay up or else."

"I agree," said another. "I'm not paying fifty pence for a look at *your* bum!"

"Yes," said another, "I only saw one tit and not even a nipple."

"If you don't pay up you won't be invited to the gym next Thursday," threatened Colin. "And by the way, it's an extra twenty-five pence for Clive because of the binoculars."

"What!" demanded Clive. "But they're *my* binoculars."

"Doesn't matter. It's extra for close-ups."

The boys reluctantly handed over their money, muttering their disappointment, "Didn't even get her knickers off."

Pam ran home and was out of breath when she greeted the girls who were sitting waiting on her garden wall. "Well?" they chorused.

"Get the paper and pencil," she panted. These were produced and Pam spanned her hand across the paper indicating where the line should be drawn. "Who's got the chart?"

"I have," replied an untidy-looking girl, extracting it from the rat's nest of her bag. Giggling, they compared paper and chart. With a theatrical flourish Pam announced: "That's Roger Worth still last, followed by James Smith and Colin. Steven Farrow and Gary Hughes tie for the biggest." She turned to the girls. "Who shall we do next?"

✈

PURRFECT COMMUNICATION

It's not difficult to decipher a cat's needs when it is sitting hopefully in front of a closed refrigerator. Interpreting a range of meows from three cats at four a.m. takes a little more practice.

You are roused from a subterranean slumber by a ginger tabby vocalising its request with a volley of meows: "I've brought you a gift that isn't quite dead yet and it's escaped and it could be hiding under the bed or in a cupboard and if you don't help me find it –IMMEDIATELY – it will probably die and decompose and cause a dreadful smell that you won't be able to track down for days. So why are you still lying there?"

This should not be confused with her 'prrup prrup' that lets you know: "I can't find my toy mouse that you've hidden because it rattles and wakes you up, so I guess I will have to swing on the curtains to amuse myself and I might even rip the voiles that you have just mended, so if you want to save yourself a lot of trouble you'd better get out of bed right now and play with me."

The tortoiseshell, on the other hand, announces her presence with a barely audible 'mia'. But this is accompanied by a gentle pat on the cheek with a chilly paw that says: "Hi Mom. Aren't you thrilled to see me? Please pull back the duvet so that I can snuggle into the crook of your arm and fall into a serene sleep while the ants that I'm covered with transfer their attentions to your bare arms. By the way – try not to disturb me as you leap out of bed when they start to bite."

Occasionally you surface from a deep sleep with a dull pain in the chest and difficulty breathing. With the frightening thought - heart attack - your eyes fly open to reveal a five kilogram pale ginger cat perched on your chest. Its motor running and its doting face staring intently into yours: "Hi, Mom. In case you were lying awake worrying, I thought I'd let you know I'm home. I don't want to disturb you, so I'll be off now to curl up on a lounge chair."

However, there are occasions when she prefers a game of chase to a snooze. She communicates this by sharpening her claws on the leather chair, a disconcerting ripping sound that carries clearly at four a.m. and one that she is aware will catapult me out of bed. The disadvantages of an open-plan layout are brought into clear focus as you try to catch a devious cat clearly intent on a game of hide and seek.

There is one noise that is instantly recognisable to all pet owners, and that is the muted, but unmistakable sound of a cat about to throw-up on the bed.

Communication is a two-way street. Now that I have learned to figure out the cats' needs, the problem lies in getting them to understand that my shrieking, "Noooo!" means that the chicken cooling in the kitchen is not for their consumption.

✈

A VIOLET HEADACHE

A look of veiled alarm crossed my friend's face. "They can be quite tricky," she cautioned.

I wondered if I had been naïve in offering to be caregiver to my neighbour's precious African Violet collection while she was on a two-month visit to Canada.

The 20 plants arrived each with their own little plastic drip tray. My neighbour handed them over with their bottle of African Violet food, like children on their first day at pre-school. After detailed instructions on watering and feeding we said our goodbyes.

I took in my charges. Some were mature plants showing signs of having recently bloomed. Others were at the nursery stage. One pregnant leaf had sprouted twins, another triplets, and a particularly robust one had managed quads. A few lone leaves were optimistically stuck into the soil.

What would be a suitable position for their living quarters? The garden would leave them at risk to the hadedas who like to come down to the swimming pool for a drink and a bit of a shower on the top step and to forage for insect life in the pots, turfing out any bothersome plants. They have already done-for a bonsai tree.

I chose the safety of the back veranda, but had to lower the blind to protect them from the early-morning sun. This did not go down well with my husband, who likes to survey the garden from the comfort of the veranda and comment on what I should be doing about the out-of-control bougainvillea.
To reduce the risk I placed several of the plants on the front veranda.

After only a few days I detected signs of leaf wilt. Alarmed, I referred to my gardening book, which indicated that the soil should be moist. A gardening friend commented darkly, "You should have been watering them from the bottom." I dutifully stood them in a tray of water.

While I was out shopping the garden services arrived. The man wanted to know what we were doing with all these violets and could he have some. My husband had the presence of mind to say NO. The gardening team use a blower. I arrived home to find the violets coughing and spluttering under a thick layer of dust. I administered First Aid by way of a gentle shower under the tap.

The following week I discovered the afternoon sun had caught some of the leaves on the front veranda plants. I took them to an indoor position in the light – but not direct sunlight - as instructed by the book. I wondered why plant nurseries don't have kennelling for plants.

Four weeks later I was dismayed to find several of the mature plants were wilted and black. I considered putting them on the church's healing-prayer list. But they could not be resurrected.

Perhaps I should buy replacements? But I had no idea what colour the flowers were – a dead giveaway should they be in bloom when my neighbour returned.

Then one morning I noticed a tiny new leaf sprouting from one of the single leaves, like a baby bird peering from beneath its mother's wing. Soon several more leaves gave birth. I was becoming optimistic. When a careless turn of the newspaper broke off a leaf I stuck it confidently into the soil.

On her return, my neighbour was so impressed with the sprouting leaves that she failed to notice that three mature plants had gone to the great compost heap in the sky.

"They seem to like it here," she said. "And as we've decided to emigrate perhaps you'd like to keep them."

✈

NIGHT NOISES

Strange, the fascination and peculiar power of a man's imagination - the terrors the silent darkness can hold. And who knows the tormented imaginings of those who have been led down the deep dark path of insanity?

Who has not experienced the childhood terrors of the ghostly monster hovering evilly in the bedroom, only to discover in the relief of daylight a coat hanging innocently on the back of the door.

Could these terrors be a kind of temporary insanity?

This is what we hope to convince the judge as my lawyer prepares my defence.

My name is Jake Cunningham and I am not, I must point out, the least bit insane, nor do I indulge in flights of fancy. I am not even mildly superstitious. Yet something happened last year to change all that...

I didn't hesitate when Dave invited me for the weekend to his uncle's farm in the KwaZulu-Natal Midlands. It was a chance to escape the hot steamy city, and the screaming police sirens, drunken shouts and roaring motorbikes. I welcomed the thought of the cool quiet countryside.

The air was crisp and invigorating as we arrived on the Friday evening, giving me a ravenous appetite.

"If we're lucky there may be wild duck or guinea fowl," said Dave. "Even at eighty-six Uncle Frank is still a pretty good shot."

There were lashings of roast beef and farm vegetables, and as I pushed my empty plate across the scrubbed kitchen table, I felt pleasantly full. The city tensions were easing out of me and I was looking forward to a restful sleep and the likelihood of shooting a few guinea fowl the following morning.

"The guns are in the rack in the hall," said Uncle Frank. "You boys can take a look at them in the morning. Better be shutting up for the night now."

The old man closed the doors, but did not lock them, and left the unguarded windows open. A born and bred townie, I queried his lax security.

"Cat's got to get in," said Frank, matter-of-factly. "Besides, no one will break in here," he added, winking at Dave, "They're all afraid of the 'bad spirit'."

Dave smiled and poured us both a cup of coffee from the enamel pot that rested on the kitchen range.

"The 'bad spirit' was Uncle Frank," Dave explained. "When he first came back from the war he used to sleep-walk. You know how rumours spread. The locals still believe that a 'bad spirit' roams the house."

I smiled. It would take more than that to keep me awake. My eyes were already closing sleepily, a feeling shared by Bulldust, Frank's old Labrador, who lay curled in his basket beside the stove.

It wasn't long before I was undressing in the enclosed veranda where a spare bed was kept for the occasional guest. I stretched out contentedly, agreeably tired, enjoying the cool breeze from the open window. Silhouetted by the moon, I glimpsed the leaves of a young willow tree swaying gently in the wind.

Presently I heard the old man and then Dave go to their rooms and their doors click shut. The cooling breeze was becoming chilly, so I drew the bedclothes about me and waited for sleep.

But it did not come. Crickets chirruped incessantly, and there was a maddening chorus of frogs from the nearby lake. The silence I had so eagerly anticipated was not there.

Then I heard a loud click. It seemed to be coming from above. Probably the corrugated iron roof contracting as it cooled. One of the many sighings and groanings of an old house composing itself for the night.

I settled back and tried to shut out the noises, but then I was aware of the steady drip of the bathroom tap – an irritating noise I could not ignore. I threw back the bedclothes, and stepping lightly over the creaking floorboards, turned off the tap. It continued to drip, so I placed a facecloth in the bowl to deaden the sound and closed the bathroom door. Easier to solve than roaring motorbikes, I thought ruefully. The country seemed to have its own set of night noises.

But even before I was back on the veranda I was startled by the shudder of the ancient refrigerator as the thermostat switched off. Grinning at my nervous stupidity, I headed back to close the kitchen door.

The moonlight cast hovering shadows on the passage walls and it was easy to see how the locals had mistaken the spectre-like figure of a sleep-walking old man for a bad spirit.

Bulldust roused himself as I entered the kitchen, vaguely annoyed at being disturbed. As I pulled the door closed, he gave the impression he was staring at a presence above my head. I must admit to glancing uneasily over my shoulder.

Returning along the passage, I felt a sudden chill, as though an outside door had been opened. I listened for footsteps, yet heard none.

As I passed the gun rack, my attention was drawn to the 9mm Mauser. I wondered whether it was a relic of the Boer War. There was also a 12 bore, but it was the Enfield 303 that aroused my curiosity. The polished barrel was cool to the touch, and the stock worn and dented. I tested the sights. The smell of gun oil brought back memories of my army conscription. I wondered whether this gun had been used in war, and if it had killed.

I took a box of cartridges from the drawer and slid one into the barrel. Again I felt the cold draught blow along the passage and gave an almost involuntary shiver. As I carried the gun back to my room, I noticed that the bathroom door I had so carefully closed, was now ajar. I must confess I felt the hairs on my neck prickle. Why hadn't I heard anyone? Had the wind blown the door open? Vaguely disquieted I pulled the old brass knob more firmly and returned to the veranda.

In the bright moonlight, I examined the rifle more closely. It was in good condition; even the canvas strap was clean. The breech opened easily and the barrel was well oiled. When I finished examining it, I carefully stood the gun next to the bed.

I tried again to fall asleep. But beneath my closed lids flashed visions of the old man, the rifle firing bullet after bullet, the sounds of war.

The wind had sprung up and the billowing curtains were flapping like sails. But in a lull, I heard the soft sound of fingernails scraping on the window. For the first time, I felt a real clutch of fear. I steeled myself to peer into the gloomy darkness and was relieved to see the branch of the willow tree gently tapping the window.

As I lay back in bed, I was conscious of my rapidly beating heart. It was not a pleasant sensation.

When I thought that at last sleep would overtake me, I heard creaking floorboards in the passage. I fancied soft padding footsteps were leaving the bathroom – but I hadn't heard the click of the doorknob opening.

There was the dripping tap again. I was beginning to feel a little unnerved as I made my way to the bathroom. Mysteriously the door was ajar. Gingerly I peered inside. The facecloth was as

I had left it, but above, staring out of the shadowy darkness, was the figure of a wild-eyed man. I gasped and reeled back. The man did likewise. With a thumping heart I realised it was my own reflection in the mirror.

I shivered violently. What had taken possession of me? I groped my way back to bed. The window gave a sudden rattle and I almost cried out as the cat leapt onto the bed. It took off down the passage as if it were being chased by an invisible presence.

I tried to steady my rapid breathing as I slipped under the covers. But as I pulled the quilt up I felt something brush my neck, like the soft questing tentacles of a giant insect. For what seemed an eternity I was rigid with fear.

The thing, whatever it was, remained motionless. What was it waiting for? Was it already injecting its lethal venom?

I slowly turned my head and would have screamed if terror had not paralysed my throat. Three leprous green fingers were spread inertly on my shoulder. I could see nothing of the creature's body.

Perspiration oozed from me. I could smell my fear, like that of a trapped animal. Somewhere in the distance and owl hooted, but the blood pounding in my ears muffled the sound. All at once, I sensed the tentacles edging towards my face.

The gun was within reach. My fingers curled round the barrel. In one swift movement I leapt from the bed. With an agonised yell I swung the gun round. It went off with ear-shattering force. In an insane frenzy, I clicked the trigger again and again.

The sound of the gunshot was still resonating in my head when Dave tore into the room and snapped on the light. I was dimly aware of the hole blasted in the thin partition wall, and of Dave's shout, "My God," when he realised that Frank's bed was directly on the other side.

Dave found him in a pool of blood. It was still slowly pumping from his head where the bullet had penetrated his skull.

I was conscious only of the bedclothes. Beneath the quilt was a woollen blanket – with long green fringing.

I now realise there is a seed of fear waiting to take root in the sanest of minds, and even in the most infertile imagination that seed can grow until it engulfs all rational thought.

But will the judge agree?

✈

50 (er 52) REASONS FOR FEELING FIFTY

It's not the wrinkles and grey hairs that make you realise how quickly the years are rolling by. It's when:

1. **You catch your reflection in a shop mirror and it's your mother you see coming towards you.**
2. Someone you consider your contemporary glances at your driving licence and remarks, "You know, I wasn't even born when you passed your driving test."
3. **The history your children studied at school is part of your early childhood.**
4. You try on two pairs of denims and choose the looser fit.
5. **You identify with Oprah Winfrey rather than Tyra Banks.**
6. The clothes you wore as a teenager qualify as 'fancy-dress.'
7. **The E-type jag you drooled over is now a classic, and unidentifiable to today's 30-somethings.**
8. While sitting crossed-legged on damp grass balancing a wilting ant-ridden paper plate on your lap and engulfed in barbecue smoke,

you find yourself longing for the comfort of a reclining chair.

9. **You find yourself scanning the newspaper despatches column more frequently than the hatches and matches.**

10. Teenagers heap the same scorn on your reminiscences of the Beatles as you did on your mother's fond talk of Vera Lynn.

11. **You pass over magazine articles about sex to read those on medical problems.**

12. When asked a question you have to 'boot up' your brain before answering.

13. **At clubs and committee meetings, you find yourself becoming possessive about a certain chair.**

14. The bank assistant you have to ask explain how the new auto teller works is young enough to be your grandchild.

15. **Your vocabulary expands to include 'thingy', 'whatsit' and 'whatsisname.'**

16. It ceases to bother you that the colours of the soap and loo paper don't match the bathroom tiles.

17. **The time rapidly decreases between when you're glad to greet visiting children, and when you're relieved to see them go.**

18. Your wedding photographs qualify for a "Brides of Yesteryear."

19. **You find what were once functional items in your home on sale in antique shops.**

20. You can remember when ice-cream was available only in vanilla and strawberry.

21. **The daring pop songs your mother threatened would corrupt an entire generation are now regarded as Golden Oldies.**
22. Younger people automatically give up their seat on busses and trains.
23. **The brush and dustpan is the only truly user-friendly piece of equipment you own.**
24. It takes several attempts to thread a needle.
25. **Fast foods mean fast indigestion.**
26. You go to the latest James Bond film and discover that Daniel Craig, and the rest of the movie 'heart throbs' are all younger than you.
27. **Your favourite recipe book suddenly resembles the battered and stained falling-to-pieces relic that your mother always referred to – the one you assumed came over with the 1820 settlers.**
28. You read articles about health in preference to those on fashion.
29. **Christmas becomes a time of reminiscing rather than parties.**
30. You ask the butcher to shred the biltong.
31. **You keep putting off the kitchen you dreamed of buying when your endowment paid out because you can't face the mess and upset of remodelling.**
32. You consider increasing your dosage of *Salusa 45*.
33. **You reminisce with your friend about the day you started school together – and**

realise your grandchildren are about to embark on the same road.

34. That time of the evening when you used to set out for a good time has now become your bedtime.
35. **You find yourself wondering why you're standing in the kitchen, and what you went for.**
36. When choosing food, considerations of digestion are as important as those of taste.
37. **When buying shoes, comfort takes precedence over fashion.**
38. Younger relatives begin giving your valuable possessions possessive glances.
39. **Teenagers serving behind counters remind you there is a discount for pensioners.**
40. You find you belong to a special fraternity of women who show no surprise when told that the interesting TV programme you are describing was screened at three a.m.
41. **Shirts and blouses look better worn outside waistbands.**
42. You have to take newspapers over 'to the light' in order to read them
43. **Your wardrobe shrinks to clothes that match your one pair of really comfy shoes.**
44. You have to sit down to put on your tights.
45. **Your grandchildren build a tree-house in a tree you grew from a pip.**
46. You start giving away your silverware and crockery.

47. **Instead of swapping recipes, you swap arthritis cures.**

48. You begin to understand the meaning of nostalgia.

49. **When your husband arrives home from work, the most exciting thing you can tell him is that the first flower has appeared on the tomato plant.**

50. You worry about getting a puppy or kitten in case it outlives you.

51. *You hear yourself quoting your mother.*

52. *You realise just how often your mother was right.*

THE LETTER

South Africa 1988
The two buddies were living and working together out in the sticks, and they were beginning to set each other's teeth on edge. Then one of them made a very weird suggestion…

Royce shifted in his chair, uncomfortably aware that Jamie was watching him read the letter.

The shimmering heat of the desert had dissipated and he gave a shiver, as much from the effect of Jamie's gaze as from the cool night breeze which had suddenly sprung up. He rolled down his shirtsleeves and moved his canvas chair closer to the fire.

Jamie's dark eyes continued to scrutinise him, a faint expression of mockery on his face. "Want some coffee?" He offered the pot to Royce.

"No, thanks."

"Too busy reading?"

Royce sensed the sarcastic resentment. It was worse after each mail drop when once again there were no letters for Jamie.

Jamie slammed the coffee pot on the fire and sank into a moody silence.

It had been six months. Six months with only each other for company. Nothing but the vast, scrubby and endless desert, under the broiling energy-sapping sun. A series of disappointing finds had also exhausted their enthusiasm. The minerals had not been in sufficient quantities to make extraction viable.

Jamie prodded the fire and then swore as the coffee pot tipped and its contents sank into the thirsty earth.

"Damn coffee. I need a stiff drink."

"Sorry old chap, we seem to be out. Perhaps I could offer you a cup of lukewarm brackish water." Royce tried to lighten the mood.

"I don't know what you're being so smug about," Jamie sneered.

After nearly two years together Royce had experienced most of Jamie's moods, including the sudden rages that threatened to break up their working arrangement as well as their fragile friendship. But this vindictive mood was new.

"What do you mean?" asked Royce.

"Gloating over your precious letters."

Royce was tired of being the scapegoat for Jamie's moods. He was tired of the whole damn business. If they didn't have a worth-while find soon he knew he could never last another six months. He rose from the chair and stood over Jamie, who was angrily prodding the embers. "I know you resent my letters, but you can hardly blame me for your failure to get any."

Jamie jumped up and faced Royce, his hands clenched, his knuckles white. "I don't want your pity." He spat out the words.

"What do you mean – pity? Why should I pity you?"

"Your family and friends write to you. You feel sorry for me because I never get any letters." There was an icy disdain in his voice.

It was true. Royce had felt sorry for him at first. It was one of the slender threads that had held together their friendship. They'd met during their final year at college. Royce had thought Jamie quiet and secretive, until their mutual interest in geology had brought them together and Royce had realised that Jamie was merely super-selective in his friendships. Most attempts at closeness were quickly rebuffed. His lack of friends was his own fault. "What do you expect me to do – ask my friends to write to you?" He flung himself heavily into a chair and continued reading.

The tense silence was broken only by the occasional crackle of the fire.

Royce was conscious of Jamie's veiled eyes watching him.

"Sell me one of yours."

"What?" Royce stared at him in disbelief.

"I said, sell me one of yours. You always have four or five. You won't miss one."

"I can't. They're my letters. What interest would they be to you?"

"So you're not prepared to let me have even one?"

Royce enjoyed his letters, it was the only thing he looked forward to – and he didn't want to share them with Jamie. But he caught the brooding resentment in the other man's eyes. "There's no point in selling you anything. What use is money here?"

"I'll swap you something." With one step he was in front of Royce.

"How about my sheath knife?" He drew it from his belt. The blade glinted in the firelight reflecting the tragic urgency in Jamie's wildly shining eyes. Royce glanced from Jamie to the knife. It was Jamie's most prized possession. Handmade by a master knife-maker it had a bone handle that balanced perfectly with the shining well-oiled blade. Jamie boasted that it could slit a hair. And he was deadly serious about giving it away.

"All right," Royce said reluctantly, fanning the letters. "Which one do you want?"

The ghost of a smile hovered on Jamie's dry, cracked lips as he made his selection. There was a look of triumph on his face as he handed Royce the knife and returned to his place by the fire.

Royce slid the knife into his belt and felt a shiver as the cold steel blade pressed through his thin shirt.

He continued reading his mother's letter. She wrote that his sister had moved to a teaching hospital and it was a pity she wasn't nearer home to help nurse his father whose arthritis was getting the better of him. He sifted through the remaining letters, but was only half concentrating. With increasing irritation he was watching Jamie read the letter, his face devoid of expression. When he'd finished he carefully refolded it and replaced it in the envelope, smirking at Royce as he tucked it into his shirt pocket.

"Who was it from?"

"I'm not telling you."

"Suit yourself."

Jamie sank back in his chair, arms folded behind his head, staring at the dark sky, his face veiled by thoughts that Royce could not fathom. The letter poked out from his shirt pocket. It irked Royce to think that he did not know its contents and he regretted his folly in making the swap.

Who was it from? Not his sister, as most of the home news came via his mother. And he'd made Carrie promise not to write so they'd have a year to decide on their feelings for each other. His other letters were usually sporadic news from friends, and the occasional geology magazine. He was aware that Jamie was watching him, a glint of amusement in his eye. "Don't you think you're being selfish, keeping it to yourself?" Royce snapped.

"No. It's my letter." He slipped it from his pocket and re-read it. He gave Royce a searching look. Their eyes held for several moments.

Jamie leaned forward and with his eyes still focused on Royce he held the paper over the fire. The corner began to smoulder, then quickly caught alight and burst into flames.

Royce leapt from his chair and snatched the charred remains from the fire.

"Why the hell did you do that?"

"It was my letter. Surely I can burn my own letter?"

Royce caught the cynical mockery in his words and felt anger well up.

"Who was it from?" He grabbed Jamie's

lapels and hauled him to his feet. "I want to know who it was from."

Jamie pushed him away roughly, so that he staggered almost falling over the chair.

"It was MY letter," Jamie said coldly. "You swapped it fair and square. I can dispose of my belongings any way I wish." He gave a snort of derision. "Anyway, what's the use of a letter once it's been read?"

Royce made an effort to keep his temper in control. "All right, if that's the way you want it, we'll do another swap. I'll give you back your knife if you tell me what was in the letter."

"No. A deal is a deal."

Royce sensed that Jamie was goading him, itching for a fight. All the bitterness they'd harboured over the past six months was beginning to surface. It was the first time throughout their relationship that Jamie had had the upper hand – and he was making the most of it.

Jamie crouched next to the fire and threw on some more kindling. As it flared the light cut the darkness and illuminated the sinister smile on his face. He glanced up and gave Royce a quizzical look.

"How about a different swap?"

"What do you mean?"

"I'll tell you what was in the letter if you give me my knife *and* your gun." In two quick strides he was in front of Royce, grinning. "It's quite a bargain if I tell you who the letter was from."

Royce listened with tightened lips. The Smith & Wesson had belonged to his father and Jamie knew how much it meant to him, to give it away was unthinkable.

"The knife only," he said, and pulling it from his belt flung it at Jamie's feet.

"And the gun?" Jamie smiled. "Don't you want to know what Carrie had to say?"

Royce paled. Something must be wrong otherwise she would never have written. He swelled with rage at the thought of Jamie reading her letter. "What did she say?" he demanded. Panting with fury he caught Jamie by the arm and swung him round, ready to put a fist into that mocking face.

Jamie wrenched free. "What about the gun?" he repeated.

Royce threw him a look of pure hatred. All his love for Carrie welled up. He was desperate to know what she'd said. He stormed into his tent to fetch the gun. Jamie's scornful laugh followed him.

"She's found someone else. Going to marry him."

Royce's eyes blazed with an icy fury as his hand tightened round the gun. He burst furiously out of the tent. "You're a liar."

"See for yourself." Jamie sniggered, as he slid the letter from his pocket and waved it in front of Royce. "I only burned the envelope."

Royce's eyes were black with hatred. Tormented beyond endurance he levelled the gun at Jamie's stomach and snatched at the letter. "Give it to me."

Jamie pulled his arm out of reach and with his other hand grasped the cold steel barrel of the gun. "It's my gun now," he smirked. He dropped the letter and it slowly fluttered down. There was a gleam of amusement in his eyes as he watched it settle on the flickering flames. When Royce realised what Jamie had done he let out a cry and leapt to grab it.

A shot rang out.

Jamie's legs buckled and he slumped to the ground, a look of faint surprise on his face.

Royce sank to his knees, his head buzzing from the gunshot, the blood pounding in his ears. Dazed, he watched the flames slowly flickering round the edges of the letter, his blankly staring eyes mesmerized by the one line he was able to read before it was reduced to ashes.

"Return your sweepstakes tickets within ten days to qualify for the early bird bonus."

✈

TECHNICAL TANTRUMS

A growing number of people have never experienced life BC (Before Computers). But there are still some of us who regard them with wary trepidation, all too aware of the serious mischief a wrongly pressed button can cause. Which is why I was standing anxiously over the computer surgeon clutching a library of backup disks containing the many thousands of words of my yet-to-be-published bestseller novels. We had just installed Windows XP and I was not about to risk losing a single one of my carefully crafted words.

It had not been my idea to change from my familiar and now user-friendly Windows 95, which has seen me quite adequately through five published books and several upgrades of computer memory. The change had been necessitated by the purchase of a scanner that would not be seen dead consorting with such a superannuated version of Windows, and an upgrade of Norton that had been equally appalled at the suggestion of working with a geriatric operating system.

With the purchase of Windows 95 had come the latest in Laser printer technology. The printer had always been comfortable with Windows 95. It liked to show off by reproducing a little picture of itself in the *Status Window* revealing where the paper was, how many pages it was kindly going to print, and in case I should wish to pop off and make a cup of coffee, the time it would take before completing its task. But it had not taken kindly to this bossy new XP system. It had not been consulted about the change, and it was not the kind of printer to take orders from just anyone. It sulked and refused to let us know what it was up to. We tried to reason with it and downloaded printer drivers from its parent website, but it thumbed its nose and kept its *Status Window* firmly closed. But just to let us know who was boss, it consented to print a successful test page.

Until the printer was appeased, I would simply have to work minus the *Status Window*.

I asked it to print out my email address book (378 addresses). It was apparent that this would be a lengthy process, confirmed by consulting the *Printer Status Bar* (not *Window* -you are paying attention?) that told me one of 15 pages had been completed. I instructed the printer, via the *Printer Status Bar*, to cancel what it was doing. But it told me it was not the kind of printer that started jobs and didn't finish them. I would just have to wait until the job was completed. It had never answered back before. Windows XP was a bad influence.

To put it in its place I removed the paper from the input tray. After waiting for it to get over the shock, I re-inserted the paper. But the printer had obviously come top of the class in memory training because it immediately resumed where it had left off. Fifteen sheets of paper later it gave a polite little burp and stopped.

When I asked it to print an email it printed a blank page with a mysterious code at the bottom - @PJL JOB NAME = 'MSJOB 12" @ PJLUSTATUS JOB = ON, before printing the requested page and then sitting back and looking smug. It had clearly been reading too many spy novels.

The computer reflects the little slots around which my life revolves. One of these is to produce a monthly newsletter for the Neighbourhood Watch. This time I asked it to print only the first page. It had evidently been doing its own research on the Web and had found a site on mind games because it printed the first page as requested – three-quarters on the first sheet of paper and the last quarter at the bottom of the second sheet. It had become a real smarty-pants.

After 20 unsuccessful attempts at printing the newsletter I phoned its parents help line. The kindly man wanted to know if I was using an LPT1 port. I had no idea. I could hear his eyes rolling (he's lucky he didn't get my spouse on the line, nearly apoplectic with rage because the email disappeared every time the **Del** (for deliver) key was punched.) The man talked me through reinstalling the inner workings.

But the printer had heard about men like that and it could not be tricked.

It had previously been a helpful, polite and well-mannered printer, apologising for paper jams, telling me when it had unfinished jobs, and reminding me when I was printing outside the margins. Now it had dug in its heels and was refusing to cooperate. It must have got in with a teenage crowd.

Finally, I told it I was tired of playing games. I emailed the newsletter to a neighbour and asked him to print it.

My neighbour arrived wearing a troubled frown. His printer was out of coloured ink and the parts of the newsletter that had been in colour the printer had left blank. When he'd questioned it, it had thrown its hands in the air and told him he was lucky it was printing anything at all, other printers may not have been as obliging. My printer must have had a quick word in its ear.

I emailed the newsletter to the company that does the photostatting.

My printer obviously has friends in high places as when I arrived at the company I found the computer was suffering from that well-known malady - 'off-line'.

It was fortunate that 19th Century technology was available. I used scissors to cut out the required parts, and glue to stick them together before doing the photostatting.

I wonder if I dare upgrade the scissors?

✈

HOW FRIENDLY A PASSENGER ARE YOU?

Are you considerate of your fellow passengers? Do you make the flight a more pleasant experience, or are you the passenger from hell. Try this quiz to see how you score.

1. When queuing at the check-in desk do you:
    a. Wait patiently in line?
    b. Know that the rope used to designate where you should stand is made flexible to enable you to duck underneath to claim a better position in the queue?
    c. Demand that you are allocated a window seat irrespective of the fact that you have a weak bladder?

2. Before departure do you:
    a. Find out where you will be boarding and make sure you are at the gate well before the allotted boarding time hoping for a last-minute upgrade?
    b. Saunter in a minute after final boarding time and demand an aisle seat because you have a minor medical condition?
    c. Wait until your name is called knowing that you're far too important to be left behind.

3. As your hand luggage do you carry:
   a. Large unwieldy curios, like African drums, and expect them to be accommodated in the overhead lockers?
   b. Fragile ornaments that have to be fussed over and stowed in a special area?
   c. Numerous bags and packages of duty-free booze and fags that have to be stowed at your feet taking up the space of your neighbour?
   d. One piece of recommended-size luggage?

4. When allocated a seat do you:
   a. Establish ownership of the armrest with your elbow, even if it protrudes into the boob of a neighbouring female passenger?
   b. Move to an aisle seat and spread your legs generously in the aisle so that everyone has to step over them?
   c. Take off your shoes to prevent your feet swelling irrespective of the release of unpleasant odours?
   d. Sit quietly and unobtrusively?

5. When storing luggage in the overhead bins you feel justified in hogging most of the space because:
   a. You are going on your first overseas holiday and need all your cameras, video equipment, travel books etc to hand?

b. You are on a business trip and your samples are far more important than anything anyone else wants to store?
c. You got there first?

6. During the flight do you:
a. Take a sleeping pill and fall asleep with your legs spread-eagled in the aisle and dribble on your neighbour's shoulder and snore like a tractor?
b. Use your laptop to make irritating tap-tapping sounds?
c. Laugh uproariously at the film and make loud comments while your neighbour tries to sleep?
d. Find it comforting to rock back and forth ensuring that the passenger in the seat behind experiences a constantly moving video screen?
e. Fold the armrests so you can flow into the neighbouring seat?

7. When travelling with children do you:
a. Entertain them by reading stories in a loud expressive voice with accompanying sound effects such as oinking pigs and chuffing choo choos?
b. Give them a battery operated game that bink-bonks or plink-plonks every 10 seconds?
c. Allow them to entertain themselves by leaning over the back of the seat and using their enquiring mind to ask the

somnolent passenger in the seat behind why he has a funny nose?
d. Give them colouring-in books and encourage them to go to sleep?

8. When the meals are served do you:
   a. Complain about the menu and demand something that is not available?
   b. Eat what is put before you without complaint even though it is not to your liking?
   c. Drink as much alcohol as possible?
   d. Consider that if anything is free there must be endless supplies of it?
   e. Recline your seat when finished regardless of whether the passenger behind is still tucking in, or that you have spilled their drink?

9. If you have a bad dose of flu do you:
   a. Board the plane regardless because you are vital to a board meeting at journey's end?
   b. Cough and sneeze over everyone, expecting clucking sympathy?
   c. Consider cancelling appointments and delaying your journey?
   d. Dose yourself with every known flu remedy, keep your nose and mouth covered wherever possible, and ask for a seat where you will be least likely to infect other passengers?

10. After using the toilet do you:
   a. Leave it as you found it?
   b. Leave it as you would *like* to find it?
   c. Leave it for someone else to clean without a trace of guilt or even a backward glance?

11. During an overnight flight do you:
   a. Prowl the aisle doing knee bends to prevent DVT?
   b. Chat endlessly to fellow passengers to help them endure the tedium as you are sure they will not be able to sleep either?
   c. Close your eyes and drift into a peaceful sleep?
   d. Ask to borrow a pen so you can complete this quiz?

12. First thing in the morning do you:
   a. Make sure you're first in the queue with a wash bag and change of underwear and have a lengthy all-over wash while a line of passengers cross their legs?
   b. Pick your nose and your teeth, fart, and generally behave as you would at home?
   c. Wait patiently until the toilet is free?

13. As soon as the wheels touch down do you:
   a. Expel the held breath that has been helping the pilot land?
   b. Start unbuckling your seatbelt and removing luggage from the overhead

rack ignoring instructions to remain in your seat because they don't apply to a busy seasoned traveller like yourself?

c. Remain firmly buckled into your aisle seat forcing your neighbour to do likewise?

d. Say a silent prayer of thanks for a safe journey and the fact that you will soon be rid of your obnoxious fellow passengers?

Score

1. a) 1 b) 4 c) 3   2. a) 2 b) 3 c) 4
3 a) 4 b) 3 c) 4 d) 1 4. a) 3 b) 3 c) 4 d) 1
5. a) 3 b) 4 c) 3 6. a) 5 b) 4 c) 5 d) 3 e) 3
7. a) 3 b) 4 c) 4 d) 1   8. a) 3 b) 1 c) 5 d) 3 e) 4
9. a) 4 b) 5 c) 1 d) 2 10. a) 2 b) 1 c) 4
11. a) 3 b) 4 c) 1 d) 1 12. a) 4 b) 4 c) 1
13. a) 1 b) 4 c) 3 d) 1

Results

1-10 You may sit next to me

11-20 You will probably feel happier travelling on the wing

21-30 Fellow passengers will probably feel happier if you travel on the wing

31-40 Perhaps you should consider travelling by ship

41-50 Hitch-hiking overland is a suitable alternative

Over 50 The world would be a more pleasant place if you remained at home.

✈

FLYING DOCTORING

Building model aeroplanes as a hobby did not seem to pose the life-threatening possibilities of say, sky-diving or motor racing, so when I confidently uttered the words, 'in sickness and in health' I was unprepared for the 'emergency run' (now down to seven and a half minutes) between home and hospital. Driving while clamping together partially severed fingers and watching the blood drain from the patient's face soon became routine.

Memories appear to be short, or perhaps the horror of it erases the incident from the subconscious, but no sooner have the scabs fallen from the wounds than model aeroplane flyers, fiddling with throttles that lie immediately behind props spinning at speeds that render them invisible, collect a fresh set. Which makes aero-modellers immediately recognisable by their scarred fingertips.

Early in our marriage, I left the flight mechanic running in a motor while I went shopping. I returned to a trail of blood which led to the ashen-faced patient, clutching his wrist. Blood trickled ominously from a gaping wound above his thumb.

"Why are you holding your wrist?" I asked, heart-pounding.

"Stopping the blood," he whispered.

I prised loose the hand.

"But there's nothing wrong with your wrist, " I exclaimed. "It's your thumb. Look."

"Don't want to look."

I told him to avert his gaze as I placed a pressure bandage on the wound, got him to hold it above his head, and reassured him that it didn't look life-threatening. I then escorted him, weak and on the threshold of swooning, to the hospital where the doctor assured him that eight stitches did not need a general anaesthetic.

Returning home, I reminded him that one should put pressure *on the wound* to stop the bleeding. But the sight of escaping blood seems to drain the senses. A year or so later I found him slumped over a blood-filled sink, his hand covered in crimson paper, clutching his wrist. Afraid of finding severed fingers, I bandaged over the paper while the patient lay wan-faced on the floor. I wondered whether I should also be packing pyjamas and an overnight bag.

The doctor discovered no more than a pin-prick. It had punctured a vital conduit in the arterial system causing dramatic bleeding. He came home rather sheepishly with a Band-Aid

But these episodes, and several more requiring a lie-down to recover from the shock, were mere dress rehearsals for the real thing - the day I had to summon the emergency services. He had a nasty bout of flu and was mentally re-writing his will. An aero-modeller arrived – he had travelled over 80 kms to buy a model kit from us.

The patient dragged himself out of bed and down to the garage - the negotiations became rather drawn out. Lack of sustenance and sudden exertion took its toll and I sent him back to bed while I saw the visitors out. On my return I found him unconscious on the kitchen floor, blood seeping from a wound on his head which he had struck when he fainted.

The paramedics strapped him onto a stretcher, manoeuvred down the stairs and off to hospital. Following in the car, I broke my seven and half-minute record.

He mended quite quickly but it knocked little sense into him.

A consolation was that a member of the flying club was a plastic surgeon, but then he moved to Johannesburg.

The finger trouble continued. Even his brother, who admonished him for his carelessness, received a seven-stitch cut.

Perhaps it is the weary doctors who have persuaded the manufacturers of the model aeroplane motors to place the throttle at the *back* of the new engines, and not immediately behind the spinning prop.

✈

ONE LITTLE PIG STAYED AT HOME

When the young troopie was offered room and board in exchange for some light work, he thought his luck had changed.

Johan Fourie became a 'cold case', his file gathering dust in the South African Police Services archives.

It has been 15 years since he disappeared. He had been gone for over six hours before the psychiatric nurse discovered his empty bed. In that time he'd hitched-hiked over 200 kilometres from the prison hospital, leaving behind the mutilated body of a young soldier in a ditch beside the road.

Dressed in the victim's army uniform, and with his close-cropped fair hair, Johan fitted the profile of a young troopie. No one gave him a second glance as he mingled with the small crowd at the Friday stock sale in the insignificant dorp where his last lift had dropped him.

An old man in khaki shirt and trousers was pocketing a wad of notes from the sale of a large white sow. Johan followed him back to his truck. He needed money to get to his sister's. She was going to pay for having him put away. He watched as the old man wrestled with the heavy rusting tailgate.

"Let me help, sir," said Johan, swinging the heavy tailgate with ease.

The old man smiled gratefully. "Thanks, son. I guess I'm not as young as I used to be." His rugged face crinkled into laughter as he slipped the safety chain in place.

Johan returned the smile, his boyish face open and honest, but his eyes were focused on the banknotes bulging the old man' pocket.

"Could do with a young pair of hands again," chuckled the old man. "Haven't seen you round here before young fella. Just travelling through, are you?"

"Yeh. Just finished my army service," lied Johan. "I guess I'll have to find a job now."

"I can give you a couple of day's work. There'll be food and a bed. But the pay won't be much. The wife and I raise a few pigs and chickens."

"That sounds great Mr ... er?"

"Dan Peterson's the name." The old man offered his hand.

"I'm Carl Venter," lied Johan, extending a strong brown hand. For a fleeting moment the terror-stricken face of the real Carl Venter flashed before him.

Johan climbed into the cab and they chatted companionably until the old truck bumped its way onto a farm track leading to a lonely farmhouse sheltered by a copse of tall trees.

The house looked freshly painted, but the windows hung at strange angles and there were marks on the walls where the gutters leaked; the old man was obviously past fixing things himself.

"Martha," called Dan. "Martha, come and see – I've brought someone home for supper."

The front door creaked open and a pleasantly plump woman emerged wiping her hands on a faded apron. She patted a few wisps of thin grey hair into place before greeting them. "That'll be nice. I've just made a fresh batch of buns. And we've got a roast for supper."

She coaxed Johan into their lounge, cluttered by a motley collection of bulky dark furniture. "What's your name, my boy? Just got out of the army, have you? Going to be doing some odd jobs for us, are you? I expect your parents will be looking forward to seeing you." She fired the questions at him.

"My name's Carl. I'm afraid both my parents are dead," he said sorrowfully.

"What a shame." She indicated a worn armchair, fussing over him like one of the plump red hens that scurried about the yard. "You look after our guest, dear," she said to Dan. "I'll see to the food."

Dan fell into a faded easy chair with a contented sigh. He gave a low whistle, the door sprang open, and an enormous ridgeback bounded in and flung itself at him. He pushed it away playfully.

"Sit, Bella!" he commanded, and the big dog obliged.

Johan shifted uncomfortably in the chair. The dog cocked its head enquiringly. Johan cautiously offered his hand, but the dog remained impassive, so he sank back in his chair.

While Dan prepared to light his pipe, Johan studied the room. There was a display cabinet with some expensive pieces of silver. "I see you have a collection of cups. Did you win them?"

"Bisley. Used to be quite a good shot."

"Could I see them?"

The old man hauled himself out of the chair. He took a key from the top drawer of a rolltop desk, and Johan noted that he tucked the wad of notes inside.

While they were putting the cups away Martha announced that supper was ready.

The table was covered with a snowy hand-crocheted cloth, and a bowl of freshly-cut flowers sat in the centre. A young African woman came in with a steaming pot of soup.

"I hope you like chicken soup, Carl," said Mrs Peterson, ladling great spoonsful of the thick creamy liquid into his bowl. "It's made from one of our own chickens. They're the best fed in the province," she added proudly.

Johan took a sip and grinned. "You can't beat home-made." He looked at them enquiringly, "It must a lot of work running this place. Do you have many servants?"

Martha chuckled. "We can't afford servants – except for Patience. She comes in twice a week. Her mother is a *sangoma*," she confided, "you know – a witch doctor." She turned to Patience, who was bearing a plate with a succulent roast. "We give her meat and home-grown vegetables, don't we, dear?"

"Yes, madam," agreed Patience, smiling shyly at Johan.

Dan carved the meat into thick, juicy slices. Bella whimpered in anticipation.

"You'll have to wait, old girl," he said, pausing to pat her sleek, glossy head. "You know you always get yours later." The dog's gaze remained fixed on the meat, saliva forming round its big jaws.

Johan glanced at the carving knife. "Good girl, nice dog," he said, reaching to pet her, but her gaze never shifted.

Dan piled Johan's plate with generous slices of meat, and Martha passed him the steaming jug of gravy.

"The meat is very tender, Mrs Peterson. Quite sweet for pork."

"Patience has a special way of preparing it. She knows just how we like it," explained Martha.

"Do you do the slaughtering yourself? Perhaps I can help?"

"Patience's brother, Thabo does it. He's very experienced. You have to be quick with the knife. If they're scared the meat will be tough."

"Will you be slaughtering soon?"

"Maybe in the next few days," said Dan, spearing another slice of meat.

"How do you like the vegetables?" asked Martha. "They're home-grown."

"Nice," muttered Johan, his thoughts still on the slaughtering.

"Martha tends them," he heard Dan saying. "She has her own special fertiliser." He winked at Johan.

"Oh, go on with you," said Martha. "It's not such a special mix. Thabo grinds the bones into bone meal and then we mix it with dried blood and dig it into the soil."

"Waste not, want not. The pigs and hens are all fed on scraps," said Dan, pushing away his empty plate and resting his hands contentedly on his round stomach.

When they returned to the lounge Dan poured them each a glass of port and Martha picked up a wickerwork sewing basket and began making neat little stitches in a tiny doll's dress.

"Martha and I make dolls for the local children," explained Dan. "I make the wooden head, arms and legs, and Martha joins them to the cloth body."

He handed Johan a finished doll.

"It's very good," said Johan. "My sister had one something like this, but the hair was made of wool." He remembered how he'd pulled it out strand by strand while his sister screamed and sobbed hysterically. "This looks like real hair."

"It is," said Martha. "We had a young girl staying with us. Poor thing had run away from home. She didn't want anyone to recognise her so she cut off her hair. Such a pity. Such lovely hair."

Johan handed back the doll and Martha lovingly stroked the hair.

Dan announced he was going to light the oil lamps before he switched off the generator. He handed one to Johan before leading him to a back bedroom. It was sparsely but comfortably furnished with a single bed and patchwork bedspread. A bulky chest of drawers stood in the corner next to a washstand with a cracked bowl. On the floor was a stained haircord carpet.

Patience brought him a mug of coffee and after setting it down on the chest of drawers she asked if there was anything he needed, pointing out the soap and fluffy red towel on the washstand. Seeing the impatient shake of his head she glided quietly out of the room.

Johan searched the chest. The drawers were stiff and difficult to open. He almost knocked over the coffee. Frowning he gulped down the strong bitter liquid.

Damn, there was nothing but clothes, some cut into tiny pieces. The jeans and T-shirt in the bottom drawer must have belonged to the girl. Pity she wasn't here now. He slumped on the bed wondering how long it would be before the old pair fell asleep. The dog could be a nuisance, unless he used the carving knife to slit its throat.

There was a noise outside the window. Must be the old man switching off the generator. He got up to look, but felt strangely tired, and his legs began to ache. He lay back on the bed, realising he hadn't slept for 24 hours. There was that noise again, a snuffling sound. But now he couldn't even lift his head. It was as if a great invisible force was holding him down.

Through a haze he saw the bedroom door open. The massive ridgeback plodded in. He could feel its warm breath on his face.

His heart was like a drumbeat. Perspiration oozed from his forehead, yet his body was oddly relaxed.

Martha's face blurred in front of him, then Dan's. Patience was standing beside them. They smiled benignly, like surgeons waiting for the anaesthetic to take effect.

A tall, muscular African in tribal dress stood at the end of the bed, the whites of his eyes showing eerily in the half-light. He turned to Patience. "Our mother will be pleased."

Johan's glazed eyes saw Martha bend over him and he felt the fluffy red towel being wrapped round his neck.

It was only when he saw the glint of the thin sharp carving knife in Thabo's hand that Johan finally understood.

A PUBLIC INCONVENIENCE

As a sufferer of unexplained anxiety attacks it has always been my practise when entering unfamiliar territory to ascertain all possible exits, especially the location of the toilets.

It was our first visit to the new cinema complex. It was one of those small, intimate affairs that are supposed to conjure up visions of fireside togetherness. We found seats a few rows from the back.

Ten minutes into the movie I was regretting that second glass of shandy.

Adopting the mufflebob, that curious tiptoeing and ducking walk one uses to make oneself less visible, I made my way toward the rear exit.

It took a few hefty shoves before the door creaked reluctantly open and flooded the cinema with sudden light.

Heads turned as I stood spotlighted in the doorway.

I began walking down a fairly lengthy stairway only to find my way barred by an external door. I had left the auditorium through the wrong exit.

This placed a panicking pressure on the bladder.

Like the phantom of the opera, I again appeared at the auditorium's rear door. I tried the middle door, again spotlighting myself for half the house.

I was on the same staircase.

I couldn't face the humiliation of a third entrance. I scurried along a passage only to find myself on the identical stairway of an adjoining cinema. Lost in the labyrinthine corridors I felt a rising panic.

In vain I sought help in the projection room – it was empty. I was starting to experience the deranged hysteria of a lost potholer.

I fled down the staircase, hurled myself recklessly at the street door which suddenly flew open. I stumbled into a deserted alley and nervously made my way into the street to find the main cinema doors firmly bolted.

I peered through the glass doors. There was no one in the foyer, but I could see a conscientious counter assistant readying her wares for the interval. I hammered on the door. No response. Desperation was increasing the pressure on my bladder. Eventually I caught the assistant's attention and she summoned the manager. He cautiously opened the door and explained that the film had long begun. Hearing my predicament he became at once solicitous and escorted me to the toilets.

He waited to ensure my safe return to my seat, accompanying me to the auditorium door, which he opened with a courteous flourish.

It was the door at the front of the cinema, almost abutting the screen. Entering stage right, I was now spotlighted for the entire audience.

Abandoning the mufflebob, I strode resolutely back to my seat. Edging along the row, I was aware of upsetting popcorn and disturbing concentration. "I'm back," I whispered needlessly to my husband as I scrambled over his knees.

I felt a tap on my shoulder. It came from the row behind.

"I'm here," he whispered.

✈

HOUSEHOLD AIDS

Supermarket shelves are awash with cleaning agents that brag about the array of bacteria, fungi, germs, and viruses they will slay. What I am waiting for is a substance that will get to grips with Household AIDS – that mysterious contagion that periodically affects household appliances i.e. when the toaster turns up its toes you know it won't be long before the iron follows it to that great ironing board in the sky.

It began with the fridge, one of those expensive imported jobs that were built for cold climates and would naturally struggle in a humid Durban summer, as we were reminded only after it broke down. The quote to fix it was more than the cost of a new locally made one, so we abandoned the old one to struggle in the garage and bought a new one more suited to our climate.

Then the car, which had served me faithfully for 15 years, began a rather alarming habit of cutting out when I accelerated into traffic. Two trips to the garage failed to cure it, and then it packed in altogether when the cam belt broke. Having fixed that, the kindly garage man diagnosed the cutting-out as a fault with the distributor and alternator, both of which had to be replaced. He was also bearer of the happy news that the wheel-bearing looked as if it was going, and the shocks felt a bit dodgy. When I drove away miserably contemplating my finances, I discovered the air-conditioner had come out in sympathy with the alternator. It needed re-gassing. Not to be out-done, the Rust-Evader had caught the same malady, but was cured by electric shock therapy. It seemed that the new alternator had upset it.

I realised too late that I should not have left the cellphone in the car as it, too, became afflicted when its battery connector broke. After having it mended, I set the cellphone down next to the hi-fi and the hi-fi clock promptly stopped.

The virus then leaked from the electrical system via the geyser, which overflowed, to the plumbing. A pipe burst somewhere in the garden and we had to summon the leak detectors and lost a portion of flowers and lawn in the search.

During the following two weeks, the toilet leaked, the garden tap refused to shut, and we had to put a new cartridge in the water filter, which also started to leak.

The infection then found its way into the swimming pool and caused the pool-gobbler pipe to break. It was only after I had inserted the new pipe that I realised I was obviously some sort of carrier, as two days later my watch stopped. (Six months later I wore it to the supermarket to remind myself to buy a new battery and it suddenly started working again. It was probably cured by bed rest).

Being a carrier of Household AIDS I should have known to wear rubber gloves when fondling the cat for shortly after, it developed an abscess requiring veterinary intervention. As I returned home with a rather vexed feline, the dog threw up on the carpet and cat number two sprinted into the bedroom, a half-chewed and bloodied bird clamped in its jaws.

At least I have plenty of cleaning agents to wipe up the mess.

✈

STICKING TOGETHER

Anyone who has been involved with building alterations will agree that co-ordinating plumbers, plasterers, painters, and carpet layers is like organising a military campaign.

It was inevitable that one of them would turn up out of sequence. This time it was the plumber, who, in turn, delayed the plasterer, and was why I ended up gluing cork tiles to the walls of the new en-suite bathroom *after* the carpets had been laid.

The tiles were my job, while my husband's input was to replace a large wooden marquetry panel over the bed. (We don't work together – it's not worth all the bickering).

I began by carefully spreading an old sheet over the new carpet and placing the ½ litre tin of glue in the centre. I was getting along nicely – measuring, cutting, gluing – when I went to fetch a new blade for the knife, passing my husband who was about to start drilling holes in the wall. I called over my shoulder, "Don't drill into the brickwork until you've found something to cover the duvet."

His perfunctory search revealed just the thing – an old sheet lying on the newly-carpeted bathroom floor. He yanked it up and spread it protectively over the bed.

I returned with the knife and gasped in horror. Glue was gently oozing from the up-turned tin and slowly spreading across the brand-new seven-shield, semi-shaggy, Miami beige carpet.

I waved the knife like a demented Sweeney Todd. "Look what you've done!"

My husband leapt off the bed and came over to stare in disbelief at the rapidly spreading sea of glue. "It's not my fault," he offered. "You should have put the lid on."

"It's glue," I shouted back. "If I'd put the lid on I may never have got it off again."

While we stood apportioning blame, the cat, which had been peacefully snoozing on a chair, fled in alarm.

The glue was now creeping across the carpet like molten larva. I lunged for the tin and righted it.

My husband, grabbing the nearest thing to hand – a toilet roll –threw it at the Vesuvius-like mess. Glue sticks. It also seeps down. It does not however, soak up. The carpet was now gaily festooned in toilet paper.

I did the most sensible thing I could think of – shed copious tears.

My husband ran to the kitchen and returned armed with a fish slice. "We'll have to scrape it up," he announced, easing the fish slice under the gooey mess. He then cast about for somewhere to deposit it. The open toilet lid caught his eye.

"Not in there," I shrieked. "What if it sets?"

The search engine in my brain hunted for glue antidotes. I raced to the kitchen and returned with paintbrush cleaner. Pouring it on the glue and mopping up with paper towels merely diluted the glue and increased its spread, it did however reduce the stickiness.

"Thinners," shouted my husband, dashing to the garage. Returning somewhat out of breath from the unaccustomed exertion, he dabbed at the offending spot, and surprisingly met with some success.

Slightly mollified, I took in the damage. We now had a semi-shaggy carpet with a 25cm round flat patch in the centre. At least the tufts were no longer stuck together. Perhaps in time they could be persuaded to stand upright.

As for my husband and I working together – we are not even speaking. And it's all the fault of the plumber.

✈

FAMILY TIES

Mavis had been so sure of where her heart lay, but now 'home' had a new definition.

They would be flying back in a few days and Mavis was still in a dither of indecision. And what about the promise she'd made to her Mam and Dad?

She had thought of the Christmas holiday as coming home to Liverpool, and Frank finally realising it was where they all belonged - not in South Africa where he'd dragged her and 14-year-old Gerry as unwilling accomplices in his quest for a better life.

Her Mam and Dad had never forgiven Frank for whisking off their grandson, and now they were fuelling the family friction by pressing to know when they would be home for good. Her Mam had even invited Mrs Blackmore round for a cuppa and to see if she could get Mavis her old factory job.

Mavis glanced at Mrs B, perched on the edge of the sagging sofa as if she suspected it of harbouring fleas. They were short of cups, so Mavis gave her the one from the kitchen window, the last of her Mam's wedding present tea service.

"Watch she doesn't drop that," her Dad muttered darkly, in a voice meant to be heard. "That's the one I soak me teeth in."

Mavis glanced anxiously at Mrs Blackmore, but she was flicking through Mavis's photo album finding disparaging comparisons. "You can't compare that blazing sun with the lovely warmth of an English summer's day... and those tropical plants don't hold a candle to a pretty bluebell wood." Mavis felt an unexpected surge of defensiveness for the garden she had lovingly tended for the past three years. Did she really want to leave it?

Mavis had promised her Mam and Dad that when Frank's contract ended they would be home for good. But doubts had crept in only days after their arrival. The familiar terraced home to which she'd yearned to return now felt small and cramped. Her friends were wrapped up in their own lives with no time or interest to hear about her new life. She and her Mam had soon fallen back into their customary squabbling, and Gerry missed his South African girlfriend. All his old mates from the estate (his feral friends, Frank had called them) had formed new friendships. He glowered, and moped and was counting the days until he could be back surfing.

Mrs B had hardly wafted out on a cloud of freshly applied Youth Dew when Frank was shrugging into his anorak.

"Are you coming, Mave?"

Frank's evenings in the smoky fug of the Crown had become a routine - out of the way of her Mam and Dad's reproachful sniping. Mavis, who had lost track of Coronation Street, and with little else to do other than bicker with her Mam and stare at Gerry's scowling face, had begun to accompany him.

They trudged to the pub through the looming fog that forced them to turn up their collars, and made them regret leaving the hired car at home to save on petrol.

Mavis sat disconsolately, listening to Frank argue about football. She no longer had anything in common with the regulars. She wasn't up on the local scandal, or what the government was doing wrong. She didn't fit in. Could she ever fit in now that she had experienced a different way of life?

Although she had grudgingly adjusted to life in South Africa there remained a haunting feeling of not really belonging, especially when addressed in Afrikaans or Zulu and it suddenly came home to you that you were in a foreign country. The secure, fall-back-on feeling that she'd hugged to herself - that she could come home to England if things didn't work out - had been pulled from under her when she discovered she was now also an outsider in the land of her birth. Where was 'home' now?

What she hadn't dare tell her Mam and Dad was that Frank had been offered a permanent position. She was fretting about this as they hurried home in the dim shadows cast by the street lights.

"What d'you think, Frank - about staying on in South Africa?"" she said, quickening to keep up with his long strides.

"You know how I feel. But it's up to you, love."

"D'you mean you'd come back?"

"If that's what you really want."

She scurried beside him, her breath coming in short rasps to avoid gulping in the damp fog, the cold seeping up through her shoes and nagging at her bunion.

Now that the decision was hers she was confused and overwhelmed with the enormity of it. Was it true that they'd have a better future in South Africa? What about grandchildren? Grandchildren who wouldn't have Scouse accents, who wouldn't know what a jam butty was.

They turned the corner to see the light from her Mam's living room glowing dimly through the thick night air. Her Dad hadn't closed the curtains properly. Her Mam would have a fit. She had a thing about neighbours seeing in, as if her Mam and Dad had wild orgies, instead of sitting watching the telly like shop dummies.

She was washing their winter clothes and up to her elbows in suds when her Mam asked caustically, "How d'ya think you're gonna get thick jumpers dry in this weather?" Mavis had forgotten about that.

She pegged them out early the next morning. But they were stiff with frost, like doll's cardboard cut-outs. She thawed them in front of the fire. But they kept the heat off her Dad, and he muttered about the smell, and accused the steam of getting on his chest.

"You'll have him under the doctor again," promised her Mam, in a tone that implied Mavis wouldn't be there to look after him.

"I'll take them down to the launderette," sighed Mavis, bundling the jerseys into a Tesco bag.

Her Mam folded her arms over her sagging bosom, which managed without the bolstering of brassiere when she was at home. "The launderette won't like that," she prophesied. "They frown on you making use of their dryers."

"They'll have to make an exception," said Mavis, struggling into her ancient duffle coat.

She set off briskly down the road, the frosty air nipping at her ears. Pity there'd been no snow, she thought sadly. A snowy Christmas would have been more cheerful.

When she returned, her Mam was doing the ironing wearing a badly-done-by expression. "You haven't told us when you'll be home for good," she said, putting the weight of her shoulder to the creaking ironing board.

Mavis took the iron from her mother. "I'll finish this. You put the kettle on," she said, aborting further discussion. Her Mam shuffled off, the loose sole of her slipper flip-slapping across the worn kitchen floor.

As if by silent consent, the subject of their return was avoided for the remaining few days. When the family stood on the draughty station platform unspoken thoughts and reprisals hovered in the chilly air. They stamped their feet and stoically blew on their hands.

Mavis recalled their previous farewell, its heady mixture of excitement, fear of the unknown, and panic that they'd made a mistake, coupled with the niggling worry of lost tickets and missed connections. This time it was different. She knew exactly what she was heading for.

Her Mam's eyes welled up when Mavis hugged her goodbye. "Mam, we're only twenty-four hours away," Mavis consoled.

"Aye," said her Dad stolidly, "But it's not the hours is it - it's the pounds."

A whistle blew and they leapt aboard as the doors swished closed. The train gave an abrupt jerk and slowly drew out of the station.

Mavis stared after the two sad figures waving disconsolately from the platform until the train rounded a corner and they were lost to view. Choosing between England and South Africa was like choosing between her Mam and her Dad, she decided. She sank back with a guilty heart, unlike Frank and Gerry, who were already cheerfully engrossed in magazines.

As they sped past the familiar backyards and attic windows she remembered the freezing nights of her childhood when she'd had to dash into the yard for a shovelful of coal, and put on a coat to go to the outside loo.

The South African Airways plane pierced the clouds and descended towards the sun-washed runway of Durban airport. The sea sparkled in the distance, and the bright blue of swimming pools peppered the gardens.

Mavis searched eagerly for a glimpse of their house.

"Are you glad to be back?" asked Frank.

"It'll be nice being in our own place again," she confessed.

"I can't wait to get on the beach," said Gerry, as the plane banked and lined up for the runway.

"It'll be good to be home," sighed Frank.

Mavis studied the eager faces of her husband and son. Life goes forward, not back, a women's magazine had told her.

She squeezed Frank's hand. "Yes, love. Our new home." A home with space for a granny flat.

✈

Printed in Great Britain
by Amazon